MINIONS

MINIONS

Ben Luten

ISBN: Softcover 978-1-4535-6902-3

This book was printed in the United States of America.

To order additional copies of this book, contact:
Xlibris Corporation
1-888-795-4274
www.Xlibris.com
Orders@Xlibris.com
86367

Contents

Chapter 1

Minions

A terrible moan, full of eternal anguish, echoes down the dark, moist corridors of a dungeon deep. The sound emanates from a shade, a soul that's done enough evil in life to be prevented from entering heaven—but a spirit that's strong enough to stay out of hell. Some shades have unfinished business, many small things that need to be fixed or one big thing. That explains why you don't see many of them. Most of the time, you can get things done if they are at the top of your list of priorities. Not only that, but it's difficult to stop a being who can walk through solid objects. The Shade's touch is a nasty thing, too. It's how they feed to stay in the physical realm. If a Shade touches you, it will drain your energy, and that makes them good allies in a dungeon that will be attacked, sooner or later, by a mage or a necromancer—someone who uses their energy to cast magical spells. Some use their ability to drain energy to create freezing cold and some of them just use their energy to propel themselves through the air faster. That's where you hear about variations like banshees and possession and the like.

That sound that you hear bouncing off the walls, that's a Shade. In this case, it's me, Jordas Shoemaker. The anguish you hear isn't the torment of the damned or ultimate sorrow. It's boredom. I don't have anything to do because I got tricked. I died outside this place, in a village that wasn't far from here. One minute I was drawing my sword to kill one of the raiders attacking us, and the next I was staring, shocked, at my own corpse—cut damn near in half by a greatsword. Problem is, I didn't have all this Shade business figured out back then. I wanted to avenge my family and friends for the wrongs committed against us, but had trouble even moving around. It took days just to learn my powers, and before I had, some demons were sent to get me. They must have been new, too, because I beat them back. When I looked into the sky I could see and feel the divine light, but I knew in my heart that I would not be allowed to enter. I went looking for the raiders to try and avenge my village and when I caught up to them, they were all dead—killed by a big group of soldiers who had hunted them down. So I'm stuck until I can redeem myself or until doomsday. So I think to myself, hey, no sweat. I'll just help a couple folks out and then I'll be all set!

Boy was I wrong. I was hoping I'd feel the balance, you know. I thought I'd simply know when it was square, but that isn't how it works. Apparently, they don't have a list of things that balance out—you have to do good deeds until you are deemed worthy. One of the guys who came to me saying he needed help was a necromancer. I asked if he could help me out in return, maybe a spell that would cleanse me or a lockpick for heaven's gates or something. He seemed positive he could help, so he has me to follow him to his lair, this dungeon I'm in now. Well, it turns out he's a big fat liar and now I'm stuck here by a magical field. Put me against any adventurer who isn't a cleric and I'll have a moderate to high success rate, but physical objects that don't have a soul also don't have energy to draw from them. This necromancer, Hebbeth The Unmarred, He's put up a big gem that's enchanted. This thing puts out a field that acts like a wall around this dungeon, and it keeps me away from the gem, too. I've already tried weakening it by drawing energy out—it's too much energy. Once I hit my limit, it isn't hard to use up what I have and then touch it again, the problem is that the field is being recharged by the ambient energy that everything gives off. Even me.

As you might imagine, there aren't a lot of good deeds to be done down here in the dark. The adventurers I've encountered so far haven't waited to hear what I have to say—they attack first and ask questions later. So I float here in one place, bored, with a goblin on the ground beneath me, whimpering. Hey, this goblin's no saint—besides, I have to eat or I'll grow weaker. I've been attacked three times by demons, each time throwing them back. Last time the assault was a pair of dark overseers, and the only reason I defeated them was because I had enough energy to do so. Those guys in hell piss me off. Quit bothering me! Like you don't get enough spirits to torture already!

There's a sound like thick slime sliding down a wall to my side, and I turn to see just what I expect. A thick slime sliding down the wall. This is Slop, my friend/pet. I'm not sure which it is, because Slop never says anything to me, but I know it has at least a basic level of intelligence. Slimes aren't known for having overwhelming intellect. Slop is a slime that is extremely flammable. I think that's Slop's special power, because I've seen it immolated and it doesn't come to any harm. My other friend is Bonehead the Skeleton. Bonehead stands next to the wall, completely still. He seldom says anything, mainly because it's hard to understand and takes him longer to say things than normal. When he first said hello to me, his word was 'Greetings', but it took four seconds to tell me that. There was one time when a cleric fired a holy bolt spell at me, and only then did Bonehead finally manage the words 'Looooooook Oooouuuut!'.

On the other hand, Bonehead's special power is extremely useful. Although maybe it's just lots of practice and not a power at all. Bonehead can pull off certain motions at an insanely fast speed. My personal favorite is when he has a working bow. One of the motions he's perfected is drawing an arrow and firing it. He can't hit anything, but he fires so quickly that the second arrow is in the air before the first one strikes whatever it's flying at. He has a few moves like that. I spent some time listening to him a few years ago to get his story, but it simply takes too long. Bonehead seems to agree that it's just not worth the effort.

We make a good team. Most of the others in this dungeon are loners, but we three stick together. Slop just ate the goblin I was saving for later, and is now glowing slightly brighter than he was a minute ago. He's a red slime, in case I didn't mention that. It's a glowing red, like embers or lava. We're just waiting around for something to happen, when we hear a new noise. Something loud. In fact, that sounds like gigantic footsteps. I look at Bonehead, then float off in the direction of the ruckus, Bonehead walking in fast motion and Slop slowly following. A band of goblins leaps out from a room to our right as we pass, deciding they will destroy us. While the dumber ones charge at Bonehead, I hover over them to get at their shaman, the only one who can hurt me unless one of the grunts has a magical weapon. Before I can get there he pummels me with a fireball.

If I were substantial, there would be body parts all over the room now. Instead, the force of it flings me backwards at moderate speed. Right back out the damn door, I realize! Back where I started, I help Bonehead as the goblins close around him, beating on him with clubs, daggers, and hand axes. One of the short, unwashed gray, vicious, stinking morons wields a woodcutter's axe like it's a battle axe. I shout and point for Bonehead to try to get the shaman as I put my transparent hand into one of the goblin's backs. Mmmm, tasty energy. The goblin goes shock still for a second, then screams in that high-pitched, gravelly voice they have. He turns around, fearfully swinging his dagger as hard as he can right through my shins. Laughing grimly, I reach out and shove my hands into him again, feeling renewed by the goblin's life force as it trembles violently, dropping it's weapon. drinking the last of the strength he has, I open my ghostly eyes and watch the little bastard whimper and crumple into a heap. Now the others have stopped attacking Bonehead except for the scowling one with the 'battle axe' and began fighting amongst themselves, trying to flee from me.

Their shaman is cursing them for cowards as he lines up another shot at me with his fireball spell—probably the only spell he has. The thud of those heavy feet continues to get louder as we finish this fight, Bonehead speed-walking forward and then rapidly swinging his sword in the same pattern. Mr. Battle Axe Fends off the first few attacks, which surprises me, but Bonehead is changing the order of his swings and scoring hits as I try to figure out what the hell I'm going to do about the shaman. I slide sideways to avoid the next fireball, but it hits the corridor wall behind me and flings me thirty feet down the hall. This time there's fire remaining, though—the floor right under the point where it impacted is alight. That's when I realize with glee that it's not his spell, but my sneaky buddy, Slop, who was under the fiery blast. The shaman is gibbering and trying to avoid the flaming puddle coming after him by running around it to get out the door. Slop stops slithering around and raises up, looking like a snake preparing to strike. The screams of the shaman as it's covered in the burning goo is terrible, but I'm sure that if I were substantial the smell would be the worst. Turning to Bonehead, I can see that this goblin is a better fighter than I thought at first. Despite several wounds it has taken from the skeleton, it has busted one of Bonehead's legs, forcing my bony pal to fight on it's level. Flying toward it as fast as I can (not very fast at all), I watched as the tough little warrior ran around the side of the skeleton and gleefully chopped Bonehead's other leg off.

I was within ten feet when it turned to me and shouts "Truce! Truce! Axer will join you! Truce!" As my eyes narrowed and I continued approaching, it shouts again, nervous but ready to fight if it has to, "Truce, stupid ghost!"

At that point I saw that the axe it held was magical.

I couldn't sense these things when I was alive, my soul in a corporeal shell. I had less sense in more than one meaning of the word. That shell blocks so much from a mortal being's eyes that it's overwhelming when you first die, but quickly you realize all you were missing before and how badly that body hampered you. As time had gone on I began to be able to detect energies I hadn't believed existed when I was alive. One of those energies was magic, and I couldn't detect it's nature, but I knew it was strong.

The goblin, Axer, (presumably self-named) was possessed of extraordinary ability among his brethren or had stumbled onto a powerful weapon and had been able to hold on to it. Whichever it was he had proven himself against one of the stronger undead I've encountered, Bonehead. I decided to stay my hand in case the artifact was strong enough to tip the scales of combat in Axer's favor. The goblin seemed uneasy which I took as a sign that we may have a good chance if it ended in a fight. Who knew, though? A goblin ally might not be a bad idea.

From my experiences, however, I had learned that goblins seem to think it's profitable and funny to turn on their allies. With that in mind I would be looking for a way to replace that axe with something less threatening to our little group. I doubted that even Axer knew precisely what it was enchanted with. Halting my advance, I saw Axer visibly relax so I figured the fight was off. My first impression of Axer was that he was an unusual goblin, though. I had a feeling we'd be fast friends. Bonehead began to speak, but I realized he was just making a threatening hiss as he propped himself up with his arms. Axer nervously glanced between me and bonehead until I smiled reassuringly to him. It felt strange to smile kindly. It was the first time in years I'd done so.

Axer spent a short time gathering the weapons of his previous allies and tore some straps and cloth strips from their clothing as well. The goblin worked diligently—wrapping, unwrapping, and rewrapping the strips and straps together with the weapons of his former friends to repair . . . and even upgrade . . . bonehead's destroyed limbs. The bitter old codger wasn't happy, but from where I stood he was not only more frightening to behold, he was also more dangerous to the next group of enemies we encountered. All the while as he worked I passed through nearby walls to find out more about the monstrous footsteps. the sounds had passed into the distance thirty minutes ago, but in a dungeon even the sound of a misstep is easily detected a long way off in the tunnels. The sound of this behemoth was easily picked up throughout the upper levels of the dungeon.

I was as cautious as I could be as I followed the imprints through the tunnels. Tracking wasn't a skill that a shade frequently used in a dungeon, but it was easy enough to follow the tracks. I examined the other tracks alongside and within the huge bootprints, the ones that would have been left by the lighter adventurers. A giant would cause a big problem. Our group of normal-sized companions would be unable to compete with the (no doubt) terribly strong warrior. Any reasonably organized party would also carry a ranger and a cleric, which ruled out my direct intervention (banishment if your a shade means you go to purgatory) as long as the cleric was conscious. It also nearly guaranteed we wouldn't be able to evade them if we were in over our heads and had to run. I suggested to my companions that we simply move in the opposite direction that the adventurers were going. They all agreed.

I didn't sense his presence until he spoke. Hebbeth the Unmarred called out, "Greetings, my minions." and approached from a route I knew to be a dead end. The faint ambient light of the dungeon shrank away from the dark spellcaster as he neared. Unlike years ago, now the sight of the necromancer filled me with a cold, deep hatred. The moment I felt the twinge of emotion, his demeanor changed. Hebbeth spoke again, his voice no longer that of the benevolent master. His back was slightly bent from delving through tomes and potions, I noted. His previously impressive robes now only impressed me as to their obvious wear and filth, and other than his attitude and appearance there was something else nagging at my unlocked senses. As he began to speak again I realized that the change wasn't *him*, it was that he had a familiar with him. Powerful enchantments had been woven over this second being to prevent it's detection. Focusing my senses on it, I could only make out slightly shifting enchantments that covered it as if there were layers upon layers of enchantments to hide it.

Seeing that attempting to discover the nature of his familiar was utterly useless, I concentrated on what he was saying, the rage at seeing my betrayer oozing off of me and—it occurred to me as I watched that I could see the evil intentions flow out of my soul and feed his powers. In my current mindset he would be a powerful foe indeed. I listened to what he said, "You will not leave this home I have created for us. It feeds off of our very essences in order to contain us all here. There is no hope to leaving—even I cannot leave—but if you obey me I will not only allow you to live . . . I will also reward you."

The Unmarred calmly explained how it worked to us. We serve him and in return he lets us exist inside his prison. He produced a wand from inside his tattered robe and pointed it at me while aiming his free hand, which had some sort of magical glove, at new and improved Bonehead. He chose me because I was the most intelligent target and Bonehead due to the many wicked-looking blades strapped to his body. I noticed that he glanced at the work Axer had done replacing Bonehead's legs. Below the kneecaps that the goblin had hacked off were strapped a small axe and a pair of daggers that were of equal length in order to provide a bit more height for our bony comrade. They also offered a threat of attack from Bonehead's legs. With a flick of his upper leg, Bonehead could change Hebbeth's title from 'Unmarred' to 'One-eye'.

I worried about what Hebbeth's wand carried. Were we encountering a more experienced and potent adversary . . . or was Hebbeth the same now as he had been years ago? Perhaps he had not meant to trap himself within his underground 'sanctuary' . . . or was he simply locking everyone in because he didn't intend to leave? Many mages consider their familiars to not only be helpers to them, but also an announcement of their level of power. Hebbeth had hidden his familiar within many cloaks of invisibility and silence. It might mean he didn't want others to know that he could only control one of the lesser familiars, or it might be some fiend from the fifth hell that could wink us out of existence with one swipe.

There was no way to tell his power, and the fact that his familiar was hidden showed that he was wise enough to know there were benefits to concealing his ally. Even lowly imps could carry valuable information or equipment to it's master, and being invisible would ensure that whatever the imp carried would reach it's destination.

The promises he laid out to us truly offered little that was positive. If he was truly such a great necromancer he had no need to grant us any reward and whether powerful or not I expected nothing in return for my services—no matter my level of loyalty. He didn't wait for our answer because it wasn't a request. It was a command. Hunt down the adventuring party we had decided to avoid and destroy them. He replaced his wand and pointed in their direction, then turned and slowly walked back around the corner leading to the dead-end. I passed through the wall and peeked out at his back as he reached the end of the hall and activated something on his person, which caused a blue-glowing swirling vortex to open before him. From it's center came the image of what I presumed was his main chamber and he began to step through, then spun and looked me right in the ethereal eyes and pointed again in their direction. Without a word, he stalked through the magical portal and the image of the room was consumed by the vortex and then the thing collapsed inward on itself, shrinking away to nothing.

I returned to the others with a grim expression. "Let's catch up to them. While we're moving we need some kind of plan on how we'll approach them.", I headed in the direction of our 'prey' and my suicide troops followed, Bonehead's metal feet perfectly timing every step, Slop leaving a light trail of . . . I don't want to know what . . . and Axer pressing his sharp little teeth together in a big grin as if we were tromping along getting ready to butcher our enemies. I couldn't help but release a depressed sigh. When our 'dead meat' was finished with us I imagined Axer's magical weapon would be the only thing left in the smoking crater.

As we twisted and turned through the passages closing in on our quarry, we began to proceed more slowly. The ground-shaking footsteps forced Axer and Bonehead to take the going more carefully despite this being familiar ground. As we grew more certain that we were nearing them, I began to pass through walls and flank our enemies, just sizing them up at first. Size was the first thing that I concentrated on considering that my suspicions were correct about them having a giant in their group. Periodically I'd howl hungrily from around a bend or an intersection they were headed toward. After a few times, the adventurers began to move more quietly—even the giant checked his footsteps so that each one didn't sound like the earth belching.

From their clothing and equipment, I determined that the giant was concerned more with direct combat (unsurprisingly). He didn't have many scars on his face but appeared to be old, which either meant he was a coward or a veteran. His equipment looked ceremonial, but that only gave me more cause to worry. Someone who lived to be old didn't do it by bringing useless weapons into a fight. Most of the time experienced fighters on the winning side got to choose what equipment they wanted off of the bodies of their foes and when they were particularly fond of an item they would galvanize it's effectiveness and enchant it to withstand damage—or with nasty abilities like Axer's axe. For all I knew, though, the little coward's weapon was enchanted to explode if he ever wielded it against a member of the royal house.

Whatever the case, I liked our chances against this giant. Giants were naturally slow, and this one was old, too. If push came to shove, I could evade the giant until it died of age. I thought about Hebbeth and decided that maybe I didn't want to try and evade the giant. The rest of their group seemed inexperienced. I got that feeling from the way they were kidding around and how new their equipment looked. Polished, as if freshly bought. They were younger humans except for an elf who appeared to be a healer or priest judging by the equipment he carried.

I tried to think up a clever way to gain the advantage on the group of adventurers. Any idea I thought of kept beginning with an attack by Slop, which would shock and terrify them. Our slimy little friend would cause terrible wounds to it's victim—in truth, wounds that looked and felt much worse than they actually were. Hopefully the attack would cause confusion since Slop couldn't really be hurt by physical attacks. As a wraith, I was my choice for the next attacker. Encountering more than one enemy who was invulnerable to physical attacks would really put fear into them as they scrambled for spells. Bonehead would be attacking from the opposite side that I did in order to negate the effect of any spell that might repel undead beings. Wielding dual swords, bonehead would have a good chance of quickly cutting down at least a few of the adventurers. I explained to my cohorts that we would have Axer wait until the battle was in our favor. I had two very good reasons for this. One reason was so that Axer wouldn't be worried about the outcome of the battle. By which I mean to say he wouldn't be running away from combat. The second reason was because a frenzied goblin screaming something ridiculous as he charges into battle naturally tends to lighten the situation with his silly antics.

I had no intention of this encounter being lighthearted in the least. Provided my plan worked, they would experience shock, terror, hopelessness, and finally death. When the team was in agreement that my plan was a good one we split up and prepared for the attack. The adventurers kept moving and as they reached the room we had agreed on for the encounter, Slop slipped off the ceiling to land over the head of one of the adventurers. As I phased out of the opposite wall of the chamber I hissed to draw their attention. They didn't look frightened at all—in fact, they moved with a fluid grace I hadn't expected. They almost ignored me completely as two of them concentrated on removing Slop. The priest, however, did not. The priest narrowed his eyes at me and whispered the syllables of a spell. As he finished speaking a gigantic ball of white fire hovered in the air above him. He looked at me and I at him, then I took a stance as if I meant to withstand the holy ball.

He smiled and flung the thing at me. I had no intention of being touched by that thing at all. I phased through the floor where I stood and the holy ball impacted on the wall behind where I had stood, sending the tongues of holy fire spraying all around where I had been. I moved forward through the ground for a few moments, then phased upward again through the floor at where I calculated to be behind the priest. It was, and his look of surprise was something to be cherished. I reached out to absorb energy from him, but as soon as I touched him I felt holy fire snake up my arm and into my chest, so I threw myself backwards from him to avoid being banished. There was no way I'd be able to feed from his supply of energy. I turned toward the other combatants to see who I would need to go after and how my friends were doing.

Bonehead was rasping, creaking, and squeaking as he moved so quickly it almost seemed a blur. With his weaponized legs he clanked menacingly (as menacingly as one can clank) as he advanced, swordfighting both of the remaining humans at once and keeping them on the defensive. Slop was slithering around now, having been removed from the head of the first victim, who was screaming in pain. The elf I had picked a fight with backpedaled with three quick steps in order to turn and see who was injured and how badly without me diving at him. He needn't have worried—he was a very good person and had holy energy filling his body. If I was touch him for very long I would be banished from the physical realm. I moved toward his injured comrade and watched his eyes open wide as he anticipated what I was going to do: finish off the wounded. He began to chant again, but I had outsmarted him. Concentrating on the weapon of his fallen ally, I interacted with the sword and partially possessed it. I raised my ghostly arms and the sword followed as if I had a hold on the handle with both hands.

The white ball of energy above the priest's head was larger than the last and he finished the last word and opened his eyes as I flung the sword at him. Their team was about to be short one healer when the Giant stepped in between and snatched the sword in mid-flight. Furious, I launched myself toward him, ethereal arms outstretched to feed and leave him without energy. I felt a wave of air catch me as I neared him and it repulsed me into the wall of the chamber. The Giant had an oversized wand in one hand—in fact, maybe it was a staff—and pointed it at slop. With a sizzle and a flash Slop was yanked off the floor and imprisoned in a globe of energy. The globe rolled over the uneven ground to the opposite wall of the chamber and bounced against it a couple times before coming to rest. The two humans who weren't injured were getting the upper hand on bonehead, backing my skeletal teammate further and further away. The Giant and the priest were keeping their eyes on me and, from the coalescing energy I saw gathering around them, preparing to end my time in the mortal realm.

In a split second, the Giant seemed to realize something and began to spin around to face an unseen danger, but only got turned halfway around when he grunted, making a pained face, then fell to one knee with a mighty crash that knocked us all down and made the orb holding slop roll further down the wall of the chamber. Groaning, he spun another quarter of the way around and smashed face-first into the filthy floor of the dungeon, releasing one last sigh. On top of the middle of the dead giant's back, Axer spat in his hands and took a firm grip on his magic axe, which had clearly penetrated the giant's armor, and with a high-pitched grunt he tore the axe free, spun it around once, and then grabbed it with both hands and raised it above his scarred and dirty head, eyes wide with triumph and glory as he shouted "ALL OF YOU BE AFRAID! YOU FACE THE MIGHTY AXER, WHO STOLE THE MAGIC AXE AND SLAYED THE GIANT WIZARD! GIVE UP NOW!"

I had to admit that he spoke pretty well for a goblin. Unfortunately the only one other than me paying any attention to him was the priest, who looked not at all afraid. His air had changed from confidence to a grim determination that made me a bit nervous. Axer wasn't lost in thought or worrying about strategy, he simply vaulted off and screamed, charging at the priest. I examined the body of the giant for anything I could possess to throw and found a few interesting items. I chose a small knife (a short sword) the giant had sheathed on his belt and picked it up, preparing to throw it into the back of one of the humans still pounding on Bonehead, but when I looked up a few seconds later Axer's body was sprawled on the ground in front of the elvish priest and the axe had slid about ten feet. As the elf unclasped his cloak and dropped it to the floor I gained understanding. The elvish priest was shaved bald in the trademark fashion of all the monk schools I knew of. I was beginning to worry about our chances against this one priest, much less if his allies had any useful skills.

Monks are trained in the expertise of hand-to-hand fighting, and that must have been what was used to either incapacitate or kill Axer in such a hurry. There was no telling how much this monk had learned about the ways of unarmed combat . . . the teachings may have been just good enough to best Axer—though from the speed with which Axer was defeated I doubted it—or the monk might be a holy terror, using special techniques to break stone with bare fist, withstand inhuman punishment, or fly through the air as if he had broken gravity's grasp. Slop was still in no position to help as the sphere of entrapment still held it and Bonehead was in need of assistance soon or the humans would smash him to dust. I lifted the shortsword, which was a work of art—beautiful runes engraved in the blade glimmered as it turned it in my wraith grip until I extended it out at one of the humans and concentrated to 'push' it as hard as I could.

The blade was hurled from my being as if fired from a ballista. The middle human I'd been aiming for had only the split second warning from the monk, "Behind you!" when the blade struck home, blowing through his armor. With a big grin, I reached down to the corpse of the giant for something else sharp when the body was suddenly bathed in a blue and white glow. I withdrew my hands from the body as if I had just dipped them in fire—that's what it felt like. The monk had prevented my further intervention using more holy energy.

Axer began to rouse and blinked rapidly, shaking his head. Remembering his weapon, he began crawling around looking for it, and finally saw it. Hopping to his feet, he made a beeline for his magic axe and I heard a sickening chop. Turning toward the sound, I saw the decapitated body of one of the humans fall over. The wounded human had gotten back to his feet despite his absurdly bulky armor, but began to back away after seeing his allies struck dead. Bonehead never hesitated, the left blade smacking away the defender's sword as the right blade thrust forward. The priest was there so suddenly I turned to make sure I wasn't imagining things. He was poised and had blocked Bonehead's right hand from delivering the finishing strike. Axer roared, "YOUR BALD HEAD CAN'T HELP YOU NOW!" and charged at the two remaining party members whirling his axe above his own bald head.

The elf's position remained almost unchanged as his leg shot out and smacked into Axer's temple, laying the tactless goblin out again. This time I watched where the axe slid to and floated over to it. Time to fling this bad boy at our impressive elf. I reached into the metal to possess it and a telepathic message came to me as I did. <Hey, watch it! Get out of my axe!>

The surprise of the telepathic message broke my concentration. Apparently the weapon had a soul bound to it. As I looked around for another object to throw at the monk I kept glancing up to see how the fight was going. Bonehead was trying to find a combination that the monk couldn't counter and the human was on his knees trying to recover. I hovered nearer the useless fighter and reached out to absorb all his energy. The monk had noticed me coming and lashed out toward me with a kick, which I would normally ignore. Since this was a very holy person, however, merely being touched repelled me. The attack struck me as a wall of air would, forcing me all the way to the back opening of the chamber. During that time, however, Bonehead thrusted at the monk with one sword while slashing with the other in a downward diagonal motion. Though the monk twisted to avoid the slash and spun to evade the thrust, Bonehead turned and kicked the human in the side with his spiky, bladed leg. Whatever the armor was made of, it wasn't very effective at stopping a slash.

The elf backflipped and jabbed his hand out toward his friend and a beam of light pulsed forth, healing the gashes and cuts his ally had just taken. He began saying something, as well, though I couldn't make out the words. Bonehead approached again, but stopped as a cylinder of blue and white light enveloped elf and the young man. It slowly expanded and as it did Bonehead was pushed backwards as if the light were as substantial as steel. A standoff ensued.

For several minutes we all just stood around looking at each other through the bright barrier between us. The human had composed himself and he and the elf began speaking with one another, trying to come up with the best plan to defeat us. They paused after conversing for a bit and then the human said to the monk, "Can you convert them or something?"

The monk didn't seem very enthusiastic about it. "What would you have me do," He asked his friend, "Offer them gold or sweetcakes? These might simply be demons, they attacked us for no reason."

The one in the bulky armor pulled off his backpack and began digging through it as he told the elvish monk, "Best offer them something. Look around you, it's two against four." The monk looked over at Bonehead and then Slop, who was free from the sphere of entrapment. He told his ally, "I wouldn't count the goblin.", but the man with the chunky armor was already shaking his head, "That goblin just killed a man who was four times it's size and uses more magic than you, Ferrin."

The elf was displeased, but he glanced around at us and decided to try me. "Why do you stalk those who enter these halls, spirit?" He wasn't condenscending, so I told him the short story of how I came to be in the dungeon. Obviously I couldn't penetrate the wall of light and perhaps him focusing on my story would distract him from the task at hand.

When I was done a gravelly voice behind me declared, "HA! Yer trapped now!"

I turned to see Axer, who began to laugh triumphantly and dance about. It reminded me of a strange dance I saw when a travelling show came to our village in my early years of life. The dancer was a dwarf dressed as a demon with ridiculously big pointy ears. Axer's ears were probably half the size and they didn't stand straight up while he flopped around 'dancing'.

The human grimaced as he watched Axer jump repeatedly and flail around. The elf didn't seem to care about Axer's victory one way or the other until he smiled slightly and asked Axer, "Mighty Axer, do you even remember how many times I knocked you unconcious?"

Axer had his back to us but suddenly spun around, enraged, snarling, "YOU DON'T—YOU CAN'T REMEMBER . . ." After several moments of thought brought nothing devestatingly clever to mind, Axer screamed, *"NOTHING!"*

Hefting his axe, our furious goblin stormed toward the elf, shrieking. I helplessly watched, already sure of the outcome. Bonehead laughed although only a spirit would recognize the difference in a skeleton's normal rasp and a laugh. This time the elf punished Axer a bit worse. Instead of one knockout punch, he executed about ten jabs and finished it with a perfect uppercut that knocked Axer right out of the cylinder of light (Apparently the protection was against undead only). The tough little goblin had scarcely landed when he leapt back to his feet and angrily shouted, "THREE!", and his eyes rolled back into his head as he toppled over backward.

The monk wiped his forehead and barked a quick chuckle. The human patted his friend on the shoulder with a laugh. Spotting the Axe that our goblin had dropped between the third and fifth jabs, he reached down to collect it. "You're trapped, though." I sneered. This elicited a chortle from everyone in the room. Except Axer and Slop. Since the barrier was still up I decided to find out more about the elf if I could. He was exceptionally smart and combat savvy—I would need any information I could use to defeat him. I wouldn't be suspicious if the information was from him—if he didn't want to tell me, he simply wouldn't. "What about you, then? It's unusual to find an elf who has been trained as a monk.", I said.

"Our kingdom," the elf said, "Has been under attack by a powerful mage claiming anything he chooses for himself without consideration for those he steals from. He calls himself "Hebbeth", which is an ancient name from a lineage that, according to old scrolls we've found, ended more than four centuries ago." His voice never wavered and the words he spoke sounded rehearsed as if he had told this story many times before. He paused briefly, then added, "He has stolen from our land for all this time. It is time for this blight on our land to end." He stopped and thought for a moment before continuing and I realized with a flash of insight that he had skipped something. He had memorized this speech and was leaving out part of the story.

"We have come here to stop him and now it seems our original plan will not work. Few wish to face Hebbeth and so we gathered those valiant enough to join us. We've searched this dungeon for only two days now and already we are only two. We will have to leave this place and bring a larger group back." A twinkle in his eye told me he had a few ideas how to escape.

"You can't escape.", I told him. "The magic emitted by the gem keeps contained all who seek to leave. Hebbeth admitted that much: even he cannot leave this place."

Axer's timing was impeccable. As the blue-white glow of the field began to fade, the little goblin climbed to his hands and feet and shook his head, regaining what little sense he had. Bonehead's unmistakable movement as he clanked his legs in anticipation of the fight coming added tension to the room again. Before the light shielding the elf and his ally left, he suddenly blurted out, "We should be on the same side. Together we might be able to find a way to destroy Hebbeth or at least leave this place so we can find someone who can fight him."

Slop slithered up next to me and reared up like a snake ready to strike at the edge of the wall of light.

I barely understood what the priest said when he whispered, "Do you want to redeem yourself?"

Chapter 2

Monstrous

For the final moment the shield was up I sought inside myself and found that what I wanted most of all was vengeance for the deaths of myself and those I loved. I missed my loved ones and wanted their company again. Bonehead and Slop struck simultaneously as I felt the last vestiges of energy fade from the cylinder of light. Vengeance and redemption were what I wanted if that's what I needed to rejoin my loved ones. Bonehead kicked the human in the leg, dropping him to one knee as he shuddered in pain. Manuevering the swords he held like a scissors, he moved to cut off the human's head. At the same time, the monk was trying to rid himself of the sticky, burning menace that was Slop. This fight was two against four; it had ended before it began. Axer charged at the monk who had laughed at him with what appeared to be a rusty torch sconce and I simply looked up at the battle and said, "STOP!"

The human raised his blade in front of his face and Bonehead's attack was blocked by it. The sides of the human's neck were bleeding lightly as the very edge of the swords bonehead wielded sliced it. The blades couldn't bite deeper because the sword raised in defense prevented Bonehead's blades from coming together. The monk had flung Slop away, but groaned in pain, his arms bloody from punching and pushing and grabbing at the acidic foe.

"Stop attacking!" I reiterated to them all. The monk closed his eyes and his arms were filled with a blue light, but it faded before his arms were fully healed and he staggered and kneeled, one hand on the floor to steady himself. Bonehead immediately took away his blades from the wounded human and stood still in front of the fallen enemy poised to strike again if I changed my mind. Slop coiled like a snake about to strike.

Axer wasn't screeching anymore, but he had almost reached the monk and was raising his sconce to strike when the magic axe suddenly bursted with a fantastically bright light and Axer flew headlong into the dirt and stone of the dungeon floor, skidding to a stop before the elf. In my mind I heard a telepathic message from the soul inhabiting the axe. <Hebbeth is our real enemy>

I was about to check with everyone else to see if they heard it, too, but the shocked looks on the faces of the adventurers and the way bonehead spun around twice checking all directions answered my question before I asked. "It isn't Hebbeth," I told them, "It's the spirit inhabiting the magic axe. When I tried to possess it in order to use it as a weapon, the soul within it . . . stopped me."

Now everyone was staring at the magic axe wondering who would allow their soul to be locked into a piece of steel—however finely crafted it may be. The voice in our heads returned, and I could feel the smile in the thought. <I am Sir Certanius of the Thoughtful Knights Of Irbogronth's Hidden Eye.> The thought stopped there for a moment, emphasizing the importance of the symbol of the knight's alliance, which was a sword turned downward at the bottom of a shield. The sword and shield also each had an open eye on them. The next thought sent images and even the remembance of sound to our heads so that his story was explained in a matter of moments.

Sir Certanius of the Thoughtful Knights Of Irbogronth's Hidden Eye was never a skilled swordsman. During training he replaced the dummy when it was finally slashed for the last time. The knights who had assisted in training those who wished to become a knight had strapped a strange bulky suit of armor to him and allowed the other boys to practice by striking Certanius. His part was to watch their attacks and learn from watching how one was to handle a blade, but despite countless hours filled with new bruises, Certanius simply seemed to be incapable of properly wielding a sword. After three years of trying to become better with weaponry,

Certanius had had enough. Feeling that his problem was something to do with concentrating, he informed the knight who was training him at the time that he intended to seek out one of the schools where the unarmed arts were taught since it was said that they helped to open the pathways of the mind.

On the night before he was to begin his journey, several figures came to him as he slept and captured him. Even a good fighter would have been powerless fighting unarmed against five strong captors—and Certanius was nothing of the sort. When he awoke, he recognized a knight he had seen when he was younger—a legendary knight—named Theodore Winkerman. He was known as 'The Pharoah' because he studied the ancient languages of the Pharaohs and not only learned to speak those dead languages, but taught many of his fellow knights to do so as well. In battle and when sending messages The Pharoah's knights spoke in the old language, and their enemies were surprised at every turn by attacks they couldn't predict. The Pharoah had always been known as having said many meaningful things, but his most famous saying was 'Disbelief is Defeat'.

The Pharoah standing in front of the young Certanius looked feeble and at first the would-be knight doubted the truth of what the old man said when he began speaking about the inner strength of a person overcoming the raw physical strength of his adversaries. Certanius finally heard enough and stood up, asking the old knight what good concentration and patience were without a sword to defend them. The old man looked at him and without so much as a gesture a wall of air knocked Certanius back into his seat. "A sword is worthless if you cannot reach your enemy."

As The Pharoah went on explaining the reason for having captured him, Certanius decided he was worth listening to and did not interupt again. The old man had studied the powers of the mind his entire life and used them to lay low the enemies of the kingdom who couldn't be reached with a sword. Having such powers also allowed him to seek out others with the an attunement for what he called psionics. Certanius had a natural affinity for such abilities and The Pharoah had sensed this. When Certanius had decided to leave, The Pharaoh ordered a few of his men to capture the boy and they did so stealthily enough to prevent any suspicions of the young man's dissappearance.

The Thoughtful Knights of Irbogronth's Hidden Eye recruited their members from those who had innate talents for psionics and only answered directly to the council of the land or to the King himself. With great stealth did they complete their missions, for many considered psionics to be a black magic. With little other explanation they began Certanius' training. The training put a mental strain on Certanius that he never would have thought he could handle. It barely fell short of torture. However, such intense training allowed him to increase his abilities much faster than otherwise possible. After two years of work, The Pharoah explained to him what his first task would be. To seek out and destroy Hebbeth the Unmarred. Since Hebbeth was a powerful wizard and could sense anyone coming near him, the Hidden Eye had planned out and built a powerfully enchanted weapon that would withstand nearly any abuse it took. They had also worked hard to make sure it was as light as possible. What they would do, the Pharoah explained, would be to transfer Certanius' essence into the weapon and return him to his body after the mission was complete.

Ever since then Certanius had been slowly working his way closer to Hebbeth.

Certanius had filled our minds with the story, and it was all over in five seconds. There was a truce while I spoke with the elvish priest about what to do in order to find redemption. "Hebbeth has caused much suffering." he said, "If you were to stop his evil it would be a great good that is done. It is a step in the right direction, but you can't expect a miracle from a single act. redemption is not complete in an instant, it's a process of proving your worth."

We weren't tired, but the elf, the human, and the goblin needed to rest before we started moving again. They couldn't just rest, though—The elf took the first watch and the human slept. While they slept I hunted and Bonehead practiced some movements. This time I went through the floor down one level deeper in Hebbeth's dungeon. My bad luck was incredible, because I dropped through in front of a ghoul that was feeding on what remained of an armored adventurer. The horrifying thought crossed my mind that if I spent enough years in this dungeon I might become the same as this ghoul—a mindless abomination feeding on the energy of the living. I should say nearly mindless, because it decided that I was apparently there to contest it's right to this . . . meal.

The ghoul leapt forward with animalistic reflexes, trying to grab me in a bear hug with it's humungous arms. I felt lucky to be an ephemeral wraith because though it only touched me I felt drained somewhat. I floated toward the nearest wall to avoid confronting the ghoul—It's ability to drain energy was far greater than mine. On the other side of the wall I paused to examine the area and suddenly heard a thud on the wall I had just travelled through. Turning around, I watched as the powerful monster broke through the thick stone wall in one more attack. Hebbeth's dungeon was heavily enchanted, and the wall began to piece itself back together, but the ghoul pounded it's way through the quickly closing hole and leapt at me again. I was so shocked by the beast's strength that it was able to drain more energy from me.

What had been a major inconvenience was now threatening to drain away what little energy I had left, which would prevent me from fending off any demon attacks. The thing advanced on me, continuing to sap my energy as I hurried toward another wall. Passing through it, I looked around for a different wall to escape through. Flowing through another wall, another, and then another still, I realized that the wraith could sense me—even though my energy level was low! It kept following me until I finally gave up and sent myself back up to the floor of the dungeon where my allies rested. It's howls were quieted by the thickness of the ceiling as I passed through back to where the rest of the party rested. The priest silently stood as I reappeared, a grim look on his face. He seemed prepared to attack.

After a moment of quiet tension, he asked, "What is it?"

"I am doomed.", I told him. "When demons attack me I must have the energy to fend them off, and I couldn't feed. As soon as they strike at me again there is no way that . . ."

I watched as he turned and sat back down. " . . . I . . . can . . . defend against them-why does it seem you aren't interested?" I asked him.

He closed his eyes and sat very still again. "Demons are nothing to fear. The only attack to fear from demons is what they do to your spirit. Demons can try to make you fear, to make you hate, to make you lust after material goods. Those are the weapons of Demons. Once you prove to them that they cannot make you fear, hate, or lust they will leave you alone until the moment they are certain their weapons will be effective."

"How would you know?" I asked, annoyed. "You forgot one other weapon they have: their claws as they drag you down to hell!" I hissed. He didn't move an inch.

"Show them your fear and your hatred and they will do what they can to feed off of it. Remember, they are spirits like yourself. If you don't allow yourself to become nourishment for them, they will leave you alone. If they gain nothing by attacking you, then you aren't worth the trouble.", he told me.

It was a bright new perspective, but I was felt so weak that it seemed ridiculous at the time. I needed to feed. Even if demons couldn't take me I had no idea what would happen if I ever ran out of energy completely and I didn't want to find out. "Let me take a little bit of your energy.", I said to him.

He opened his eyes and looked at me. I could tell he was considering whether or not he wanted to allow me to do that. After a pause he said, "Very well."

Famished, I floated next to him and began eating his energy. I was surprised how long he allowed me to feed—he had a great deal of energy. I was still hungry when he said, "Enough.", but I didn't press my luck. <Interesting.> Certanius chimed in. The form of his thought made me feel like he was accustomed to being bored. I gave the axe my best annoyed look. <There was something about your story I wanted to clarify.> he told me. I listened as he sent telepathic messages to me. 'Hearing' telepathy is more a feeling than anything else. The message has already been formed and sent, all you have to do is catch it. <You said earlier that you were denied vengeance when the soldiers slaughtered the raiders. The raiders were gathered and sent by Hebbeth. That's not the only thing, either. A short time—remember I'm thinking of time by my standards—after he had sent the raiders he received a large boost in the number of minions guarding his dungeon. I think you weren't the only one recruited after the raid and subsequent slaughter. It appears to me as though it was planned out.>

The scenario did ring of truth, one had to admit. I tried my hand at a telepathic message and he seemed to have received it without problem.

<Yes, I think that several if not most of the undead guarding this dungeon were either villagers or raiders. You may yet have a chance for vengeance, if you are still of a mind to accomplish that.>, Certanius told me. "How will I recognize which ones are which?" I asked him. He responded almost instantly, <The only way to recognize them is through their actions.>

I was both thrilled and terrified at the news that my friends and relatives might be bound in this place. My thrill was to know that I now had a more noble cause than revenge: saving those I loved from being trapped in this place. My terror was for the thought that some of them might be imprisoned here. It made me a lot more determined to kill Hebbeth, knowing there were more people depending on his destruction than myself and a few new allies. I felt the weight of responsibility on my shoulders from this knowledge. If I failed, things might happen that were so bad that the word horrible wasn't enough to describe it. <If you can help me to reach Hebbeth, I assure you I will end his reign of evil. I just need your help to reach him.>

I nodded toward the axe and he added, <Please trust me if I ever ask you to do something and you don't understand why. I will never misguide you.> I was taken by the knight's solemnity and straightforwardness. I didn't know what else to say to that except to tell him, "I will help you."

We talked about our families while they others slept, even Slop. The little slime became eerily still when it slept. Bonehead stood a short distance away, the only sound heard from him the whisper of blades unceasingly slicing the air, preparing for battle.

When everyone was rested we took a large staircase a moderate walk away to reach the next level down in the dungeon. We entered a large room with little light in it and Certanius glowed bright enough to grant us light with a soft blue luminescence throughout most of the large chamber. The other end was shrouded in darkness but for a pair of green eyes that watched our group. It watched for a few seconds and then began shambling forward, coming into the light to be revealed as a zombie. Our group had entered quietly but we all prepared to smash this zombie into dust—a single zombie was hardly a challenge for an entire group like us. While the rest of us prepared to attack the undead if it neared us, Bonehead reacted first.

With naught but a whisper and one clank of his feet as he landed he whipped both blades around side by side and decapitated the zombie before it could so much as turn to face the skeletal swordsman. Even it's head thudded dully, leaving the room in relative silence compared to it's shambling. "That was EASY!", Axer shouted, running up and kicking the head into the dark end of the room. As the head quit rolling we realized that a sound stopped that we simply hadn't noticed at first. Multiple pairs of green eyes turned away from what they had been looking at and began bobbing and sliding forward. Out of the darkness came two, then five, then more zombies. Then a few more. Big zombies, small zombies, mostly fat zombies. They were covered in blood and a few of their mouths dripped gore. If I had had a stomach it would've turned twice. I turned and looked at the priest and he said, "No." without even looking back at me and then he turned and exited the room by way of a large doorway.

The rest of us followed suit. Axer looked shocked at us and the Human adventurer asked, "We can handle some zombies, right?", before shrugging and leaving the room to follow us. I should say he followed them, because I am the slowest of the group, so even Axer passed me. I heard Bonehead's explanation to the Human as we followed the priest, "Waaaaaaaaaaaaaaaassssssssssssssssted . . . Tiiiiiiiiiiiiiiiimmme".

After two more turns we slowed. Zombies weren't known for their perception or brains. "Help me . . . please." and a sob drew our attentions. A badly injured young maiden lay against the wall, sobbing. The adventurer—who I called the adventurer due to the equipment he lugged with him—ran to her to help mend her wounds. "You've got to use some healing, help her!" He sounded frustrated at his wise companion as he neared the woman. Bonehead began rapidly clanking toward her and the priest stopped him with an arm outstretched. I began to wonder if he was thinking clearly when he motioned for the Human to help her near to him. I held my silence since he had given pause to begin with, though. The Human brought her to the priest and she leaned on him for what I'm sure she hoped we thought was support. It was a long shot to capture and escape with one of the men, but the vampire must have been desperately hungry. I was watching the priest waiting for some sort of devestating holy energy attack to vaporize her, but I was as surprised as her when the lethal attack came not from the priest, but the adventurer behind her.

The old fashioned vampire remedy: the stake to the heart. It was a masterfully executed execution—with the exception of the priest's performance. She should've seen the way he halted in his tracks upon noticing her there. Her eyes widened in shock and she convulsed twice before her body fell over. As she 'died', she opened her maw to reveal a huge pair of fangs, and she managed to snap her mouth shut and regain her "poor helpless maiden" appearance before she fell over. The Priest backed away from the awful, bloody mess and used a dab of holy water on his head, his compatriot's forehead, and then the vampire's forehead. "We need to make sure this body does not return.", the priest told the packboy. The adventurer and he locked at each other with a spark of insight in their eyes and both simultaneously said, "Zombie food." They both giggled most unprofessionally as the Adventurer hefted the corpse and headed back to the zombie chamber. "Why feed them?" I asked the Elvish priest. He seemed to be meditating for a moment and then I saw the blood vanish from his clothing before he explained it to me. "I would rather face a room full of zombies than one vampire." He said. Personally I think he underestimated how much trouble a room full of zombies could give a little group like ours, but for now the reasoning was sound—we could easily lose the zombies if we needed to.

It didn't take long for our zombie caregivers to return and we moved onward. I had been on this level only once, and that's when I had encountered the huge ghoul that had nearly doomed me. Suddenly I realized how appropriate it would be to share my experience with my allies. I called a halt and told them. The adventurer unslung his pack and pulled out a few small strangely shaped vials. The vials were formed with many tiny rounded curves in the glass. I assumed they were weapons of some kind designed to burst on impact. I was beginning to be impressed by our fully-equipped adventurer as he prepared for larger foes. When I was done telling them about the monster the priest smiled and glanced at the man who was carefully sliding the vials into his belt and told us, "That's why I don't waste my holy magic on zombies."

The two men and Axer took advantage of the break and ate some food as well. Slop ate a few bugs and then we moved out again. The Adventurer had donned a pair of boots that glowed even more brightly than Certanius. I was beginning to envy his foresight and was starting to get curious about his name as we continued. The adventurer halted us with a grunted, "Wait!" and examined one of several necklaces he had on. He turned a slow circle and then faced the archway we were standing in front of again. He tucked the amulet away and picked up a few loose stones from the ground, then threw one of them through the archway. As the rock reach the archway it slowed suddenly in midair and in the blink of an eye there came the sound of metal on stone. As if underwater, the rock split into two halves and each half flew in opposite directions. As they reached the edge of the arch they returned to their original speed and fell to the ground.

He threw a second and third rock with the same effect, and then examined one of the halves that had fallen. "Sheared through as cleanly as scissors cut cloth.", He noted. Our pack rat was brooding to himself until the elf asked, "Can it be passed?"

"It certainly can." he said, and I expected him to produce the item that would deliver the answer. "Unfortunately,", he told us, "I didn't bring along that ring."

He looked embarrassed, but I wanted to know, "Why not?"

Removing his gloves so that we could see, none of us blamed him. Some of his fingers had two rings, which was impressive since magical abilities based on different elements tended to cause discomfort. Discomfort as in people have lost hands, exploded, turned into different animals, and been teleported to locations that have yet to be found. Perhaps they teleported to someplace crazy like the middle of the ocean or in the wall of some castle. Our friend had no doubt spent a long time studying the effects of different spells to learn their base element and then most likely spent a longer time finding the rings with the spells he needed. Those rings aren't cheap.

"You must have been very wealthy.", I said with admiration.

He smiled sadly, "I was . . . I was."

He sighed and shook himself out of it, forgetting his regrets and returning to the problem at hand. "This is generally referred to as a speed trap. It's designed to kill people who enchant themselves with haste at a very powerful level in order to get through this area quickly." He turned to us and then chuckled before continuing. "An unfortunate side effect is that the trap that's built to kill someone moving at that speed also kills anyone who attempts to pass through it at a slow speed. Or, in fact, at any speed."

The elf asked, "Can't you cast a spell on the trap to slow it down so that we can get through?"

The adventurer shook his head and sat down, digging through his pack looking for a way to bypass it as he answered, "Not a chance! The enchantment inside the archway greatly slows whatever is inside it—and all we saw of the blade was a wink of metal. The blade itself is moving much too fast. Since it's a combination mechanical and magical trap It probably doesn't require an outside power source. If you're already going to enchant the blade with that much magic you might as well save the time on building the mechanisms and just make a blade spin extremely quickly on a rod that falls when somone passes the arch." He pondered for a moment, then returned to searching his pack for the solution to the riddle.

"Is there a way to keep the rod from falling? How does the trap detect when someone is in the archway?", I asked. He didn't look up when he answered, "The eye of the trap is usually the genius element of the trap. It's not impossible to find, but unless you can see through cloaking enchantments don't expect to find it. It could be a dark-detecting blade as easily as the archway might detect movement. The eye could be an ear. Perhaps it's just in range so that when you reach that point the ear senses the sound you make and activates the blade. If I had my choice, it would be to find a way to destroy or disable the trap rather than try to find the shadow of the ghost's breath."

I floated over to the archway and everyone watched as I stuck a ghostly arm through. It wasn't wet, but it felt like I was moving my arm through very thick goo. When my arm reached the point the rock had been at when it was sliced I saw the flash of metal and felt the blade pass through my arm. The room before me was flashing. The blade was moving faster than thought, repeatedly attempting to sever my ethereal arm at the elbow. Whatever the eye of the trap was, it wasn't fooled by someone being spectral. That proved to be a weakness, though. The adventurer clapped once and pointed at me, "HA!"

He closed his backpack and slung it back over his shoulders. "Stay right there.", he told me. I shrugged and decided to focus on something other than the next room, which was a flashing blur, so I stood there and watched him. He dramatically slipped one vial from his belt and struck a pose, tossing the vial lightly at the lightning-fast blade. As it entered the archway I saw the bubbles playing inside the container for a few seconds and then the blade struck the vial and the green liquid slowly sprayed in all directions. The adventurer's eyes widened suddenly in terror and he shouted, "COVER!" and defended his face with his arms. Bonehead either assumed he wouldn't be affected or was caught off guard, Slop began to slither backwards and at the last moment the elf held out his arms and closed his eyes. The green fluid droplets left the zone of slow movement as if spewed from a Blacksmith's bellows, and the only two left undefended by the elf's shield were myself and Axer. After the initial contact, there was a moment of silence.

Gradually it was replaced with a sound like insects that became louder and more pronounced: the sizzle of acid. Axer slapped at one arm as if vanquishing a pesky bug, then slapped it again and then the other. Finally, he raised both arms and looked in wide-eyed fear at smoke begin to rise from them, flesh quickly vanishing from the spots touched by the terrible stuff. The elf was preparing a healing spell already, but Axer screamed and threw himself to the ground, rolling in pain and (mostly) horror. He curled up in defeat and looked up at the human and raggedly asked, "Please give me a present . . . before . . . . I . . . . die . . ." The human cocked an eyebrow in mild amusement and looked at the elf, who was almost done with the healing spell. The priest noticed the movement in the corner of his vision and turned and looked at his friend's bemused expression. The priest choked off a laugh and the healing spell's energy began to disperse.

Axer turned to me next and whispered, "You're scary." and then flopped over on his other side to speak to bonehead. His arms flopped lifelessly and priest and packman were having trouble containing their mirth. Weakly, he told bonehead, "You take my axe. I still hate you. Kill elf to avenge . . . . soul . . ." and with that, Axer closed his eyes, stuck out his tongue, twitched no more than four times (I was proud) and 'died' with a deep exhalation.

Our amazing duo were snickering uncontrollably—I guess Axer thought they were crying. The priest raised his hands solemnly over Axer and declared, "Our own mighty Axer has fallen in battle. It was a shame none of us could save him even though he was a disgusting little runt that got knocked out four times at my own hand." I even found myself grinning as Axer did exactly what we all expected him to do. He yelped and jumped to his feet and ran over to the elf, punching the hysterically laughing elf in the shins and angrily declaring, "HEY, IT WAS THREE! THREEEEE!"

The elf deftly tripped Axer, who bonked his head on the ground and yelped again, "YOWCH! STUPID BALD ELF!" Axer got back to his feet with a furious look in his eyes and took what I can only assume is a type of goblin fighting stance. I really can't describe it. We were all enjoying the joke on Axer when a sound like a million swords whittling down a mountain clawed the air like the devil's own scream. When we were all done flinching—our mortal comrades for the pain in their eardrums and we for the thought of their pain—we all looked back at where the lightning blade had been. We examined the floor of the archway from a safe distance and found a slit about the size of the lightning blade's length and width. The adventurer mumbled something about his acid and the centrifugal force of the blade or some such nonsense. Throwing rocks and having me stand in the middle of the archway produced identical results—the blade was no longer functioning. Although it took a few extra minutes and a heavy dose of tension, the entire group made it through the archway without anyone being chopped in half.

Certanius hadn't projected any thoughts in quite a while, but as soon as I began to wonder if he was still with us and alright he assured me, <I am quite alright. You should worry about that wraith.>

Certanius had attached some sort of psionic arrow to the telepathic message because I knew exactly which direction to look. Through the archway, the monstrous wraith that had nearly drained me of all energy was charging toward us. I was chilled at the fact that we hadn't heard it sneaking up on us and panic gripped me as the thing entered the archway and continued coming for us, albeit at a fraction of it's normal speed. Suddenly the reason for the archway was clear—to trap the gigantic energy vampire!

Bonehead clanked over and stood in front of where the beast would emerge with his blades poised at it's eyes. The room we were in was medium-sized with a large entrance that opened to blackness. The stairway down descended into the dark. The adventurer commanded us back and the elf began to prepare what I hoped was his mightiest holy spell. "What is your name?" I asked the human. He had strapped most of his items to his person and discarded his backpack in the corner of the room. Pointing one of his hands at the floor around Bonehead, he unleashed some of the combined energy of his water-element rings into a frozen layer over the floor. "Nigel Shepard," he told me, "Ringmaster.", he grinned as he finished his icy impediment. I looked over at Axer, who seemed to be . . . meditating?! As I watched he opened his eyes and smiled at me with his mouthful of wickedly sharp teeth. An aura of white seemed to outline him. Ringmaster focused on the oncoming beast and aimed a beautifully crafted blue glowing wand at it.

I wondered if I was mad or if one of the magical effects was giving off a buzzing sound. The monster didn't scream as it reached the edge of the archway and had it's eyes stabbed by Bonehead's blades. It tumbled forward on the ice and crashed to the ground, sliding forward. For a moment, we slowly scooted away from the wraith's prone form. one of bonehead's legs stuck out from underneath our huge enemy. The dread came right before it began to rise again. The wraith pulled the ends of the sword-hands out of it's eye sockets, which seemed to writhe disturbingly. "It's regenerating!" I shouted at the others, "Attack before it can see!"

Ringmaster loosed the spell he'd been powering up with his wand—and nothing happened!

Axer gleefully followed my request to harry the wraith, hacking and slashing using Certanius' embodiment to tear gouges from the wraith's stomach, legs, and he even slashed off a couple of the cruel looking clawed digits from it's hand. I saw one of it's eyes fully form and it used the arm with the shredded hand to bat Axer into the wall next to the archway. There was a loud smack and Axer's body hung in the air half a second before thudding to the ground. With the force taken to fling Axer into the wall, I was sure the goblin was dead. I was staying away from the looming foe as it turned to face the priest. It crouched, prepared to leap aside and avoid the massive orb of holy energy the priest was ready to propel at it. With perfect timing, Nigel extended both fists together and a burst of scalding steam lashed out, reddening the pale flesh of the giant ghoul and causing chunks of undead flesh to slough off. The attack angered the monster, and it turned and stepped twice toward Nigel extending it's hand to grasp and crush the puny human. Again, with perfect timing, Nigel's first attack struck the beast—a fantastically bright flash of lightning as a magically formed super bolt tore into the top of the wraith's head and flowed through it's body to the water-covered floor. The electricity ripped through the wraith, gripping it's quivering body like the hand of an angry Zeus.

While the wraith was stunned our priest hurled the ball of holy energy into it and the Ringmaster continued to pummel the resilient foe with magical spells that he timed with such precision I was amazed. Great tongues of flame leapt from his left hand, which was covered in rings of gold and iron, and immolated the fearsome beast in fire. Nigel's hands seemed to each operate independently of one another. He ended his stream of fire and simultaneously cast another charge from his super lightning bolt wand. His left hand slipped another vial of acid from his belt even while he tucked his wand away with his right hand and reared back to throw the vial of acid at the monster. The flames had almost gone out already when the holy energy struck the beast. Now it roared in pain as flames of white fire clung to it and vaporized it's flesh even as the ground remained unsinged. Evil black fumes seeped out of it, and where the dark energy met the light, it was dispelled. The burst of holy energy did tremendous damage to the wraith, but faded before the terrible thing was finished. To my shock, Axer tumbled into the back of the monster hacking and slashing away, not so much as a bruise on his head from the impact of striking the wall. He still glowed white with some sort of protection Certanius granted him.

The fiend spun it's huge body around after only a few slashes and plucked the brave, stupid goblin off the ground. With a rumbling hiss of hatred it held the goblin up to it's face and unleashed an unexpected attack of it's own: it's maw opened and sinister black smoke rolled out of it's open orifice, enveloping Axer's upper torso completely. Another bolt of holy energy burned into the wraith's lower back and—finally—it staggered. Nigel threw the acid vial into the evil behemoth and it growled like half the demons of hell, the sound not only heard but felt. It spun and turned the screaming, gurgling goblin into a missile of it's own, and for once Nigel froze with indecision. The goblin spear knocked him out and Axer bounced off the wall onto the ground making sounds that suggested he was caged in an unimaginable nightmare. I hoped whatever the evil cloud did to Axer that the it wouldn't break the little fighter's spirit. The elf unfortunately spent too long observing the results of the monster's marksmanship and it roared triumphantly as it fell on him sweeping it's cruel claws back and forth trying to rend him to pieces.

I would not have accepted the wager if someone had bet that our elf would be torn apart in less than ten seconds.

I began to approach the monster in the hopes that it would be spending too much energy to regenerate and thus allow me to overwhelm it's energy stealing ability and weaken it further. The elf was still screaming in desperate rage as I stuck my ethereal hands inside the vicious fiend. The speed at which it snapped straight up tipped me off that it had noticed. In fury it turned it's attention to me and began fighting to draw more energy from me than I did from it. What worried me was that I could tell the regeneration stopped, so it was going to use it's remaining energy to suck as much as it could from me. The first time we had met it had won easily, but the first time we met it had just fed and I was low on energy. The tables were tilted in my favor now, and as I felt the pull on my energy begin to weaken I knew I would destroy it if only there was a way to keep the evil being from breaking off and running. The wraith's cunning was obvious from the first time I had encountered it, and I had little hope of it facing me in a struggle to the death. It broke from our struggle for energy and loped off toward the archway to escape. I moved too slowly to catch it. "NO! FINISH IT!", I cried out to my allies but they were all incapacitated. Only one of them heard me, and it fell on the wraith's head moments from the archway.

Chapter 3

Rats!

Slop ferociously tried to devour the wraith to no avail. Despite the impediment of an acidic slime on it's stabbed, busted, shocked, burned, exorcised head the wraith entered the archway. Taking stock of the situation I examined Nigel and found that other than having his head busted by a flying goblin he just needed to be roused. He winced every time he turned his neck but otherwise seemed alright. He almost fell over as he rose to his feet the first time. Steadying himself for a moment he went over to heal the monk the old fashioned way, bandages and medicine. The elf was awake, but drowsy and in great pain, his clothing and body bearing gashes from the massive claws of his assailant.

Axer had stopped flailing around and screaming and the black cloud that clung to him was diminishing quickly, revealing the damage. The goblin's red-brown hide from his toes to the bottom of his stomach was normal, but the thick skin melded into a less savory color and texture above that. The cloud of evil had drained most of the life and energy from him, leaving his body gaunt and his flesh cracked and bloody. He was breathing, but it was shallow and scratchy. Once the elf was propped up against the wall and resting Slop came slithering through the archway and we roused Axer. "You going to be okay, Axer?" Nigel asked him. His lips moved slowly but his voice failed him until Nigel gave him some water from a canteen hung by the weary adventurer's shoulder. We looked at each other as Axer drank and drank from the canteen as if he were dying of thirst. Once he stopped he cleared his throat (I noticed Nigel had to swallow his nausea at the sound Axer's voice made when cleared) and said, "Where . . . axe?"

Nigel gave Axer a vial of medicine and the goblin made a disgusted face as he first tasted it, but then realized it had been sweetened and eagerly finished it off, begging another vial out of Nigel. "I think he'll be fine.", Nigel said.

"Why . . . so . . . dark?" Axer carefully, slowly pronounced each word. Nigel and I looked at each other and back at Axer. We both realized at the same time that Axer had lost his sight. There were far off screams echoing from somewhere, as if several people had been driven insane with fear. It was constant and barely audible. "Axer," I informed him, "I think you've lost your sight."

The goblin took several seconds to absorb the information and said, "No." with a smile. When neither of us responded the smile broke, "No! NOOOOO!", he began to sob. After a short time we located and handed him Certanius and he slowly quit crying and was asleep in ten minutes. He was still better off than Bonehead. The old skeleton had been smashed to dust by the huge monster that fell on him.

We rested for a couple hours and then I woke them and we moved down the dark stairs to the next level. Nigel tore a piece of cloth from the elf's torn up shirt and left three vials and some sort of magical charm tucked under the ripped cloth in front of the archway. "What exactly will that do?" I asked our ingenius ally, the Ringmaster. His face was grim and he raised a closed fist, then dramatically, quickly opened his hand. It reminded me of an explosion, so I took it that's what he meant and nodded my approval. We spoke not at all on the descent of that shadowy spiral staircase. It was so empty and long I kept expecting something to attack us but nothing did. We had travelled the incredibly long staircase for ten minutes when we felt a slight rumble. I looked at Nigel and he smiled and made the same motion with his hand as before. Kaboom.

I was sure it would slow the bastard down, but our entire group had hit it with everything we had and it had still severely wounded most of us and destroyed bonehead and STILL escaped. I was afraid we would be seeing more of the giant wraith. Grates appeared as we continued lower, and the steps became a slide which ended in water up to our waists (Axer's shoulders). There was an incline that rose up and the floor became dry again while we went down the long hall. We came to an intersection of five halls including the one we had just come from. It was very . . . moist. A droplet of clear slime plopped onto Ferrin's head and he wiped it off and dried his hand on the side of his pants with the extremely accurate observation, "Yewck". The stench wafting through these halls was very bad according to our living comrades, who covered their noses and mouths. The floor was coated in something red and slick. There were lots of bugs—bloodsuckers—flying around, and although Slop was eating well the little bugs that swarmed our friends began to drive them crazy with aggravation. "That's a good way to throw off a mage's concentration" I thought aloud. "Genius, really. A self-sustaining spell disrupter." Nigel stopped us and went ahead a short distance and then wasted some of the energy in his fire rings to burn a bunch of the little pests up. Before long the monk put a stop to it, "That's enough. Don't forget we have bigger fish to fry. You had better save the energy in your items in case the wraith catches up to us." I got a bad feeling that there was something bad coming our way (and it wasn't an insect) and an even worse notion that I was sure to find out what it was much sooner than I wanted to.

That simple reminder was enough to make anyone paranoid about wasting energy. We had only been on that foul, humid floor for ten minutes when we heard something large coming our way, the pounding of it's paced footsteps causing us to get ready to fight again. We had defeated the wraith from hell, what could challenge us now? Axer cried out a battle charge and ran into the wall. Okay, I thought to myself, chagrined, maybe we should consider evasion.

The pounding steps were rapid and consistent. One thing was for certain: there was no way we would be able to outrun it. Ringmaster woke Axer and our monk charged up a spell and held it in his hands waiting for our foe to come into view. Our clever adventurer tied a rope to axer so that he could run with us without needing to hold hands. As the sounds came closer there was a noticable 'crunch' every time there was a footfall. When it turned the corner we found it was not a huge wraith. The creature was a humanoid shape and appeared to be made of blood, viscera, filth, and chunks of gore. Every movement it made splattered tiny chunks of it's body everywhere. Even the supreme will of the elf was no protection against the horrendously vile enemy. He face had paled white and he was gagging, yet he was the best of our living friends. Axer was shaking dreadfully and, right before vomiting, said, "The smell is . . ." (gasp), "So bad! Smell so bad! Is it . . . evil crap monster? Smell like . . . elf! hahaha-" at that point he gurgled and lost the last meal he'd eaten. Ferrin simply puked in response. There was a plop of slime not far off.

I had heard of gore golems in some of the tales brought back by the dungeon delvers who had shown up in our little village's pub. I hadn't heard much, though. The consensus was that it wasn't good manners to speak about those monsters while someone was eating or even drinking. Besides, from what little I had heard it sounded like they would rather forget the encounter.

This gore golem didn't attack us, however. What I mean is that it did not begin swinging it's large arms to pummel us. In fact, it never stopped and didn't seem to detect us. Until it's mouth opened. The stench that was so horrible must have become hellish—my sickened allies puked until they had nothing left to puke and then began to heave. As if it hadn't already proved that it could nauseate even the most dedicated minds, it then proceeded to projectile vomit part of it's mass onto all of our living adventurers. The sight was so disgusting that I turned away, hoping that someday I could forget the vile image. The golem, having completed it's job, did not remain to fight. It just stomped off down the corridor. Not exactly deadly, but certainly painful to the senses.

My teammates tried to compose themselves and get as much of the awful stuff off of them as they could. That was when we heard something else coming from the hall that the golem had come from. Knowing we were in no shape to face another threat I checked around the corner to see what was on it's way. I hadn't been wrong when I thought it sounded like a thousand tiny claws. The sound came from piles and piles of black rodents twice the size of a fist. I turned and saw my comrades, covered in blood from head to toe. I got the idea.

"RUN! RUN! GO!" I shouted at them as the black wave approached. Ringmaster, Axer, and the elf began stumbling away from the corner. "If you want a thousand reasons to *RUN*, look back!", I bellowed at them. They did and when the hall filled with carrion rats they took a moment to comprehend as I had. Carrion rats are just simple rodents and only eat from the dead or dying. However, the gore golem had done a good job of tricking the carrion rats. Ringmaster stood a little straighter when he saw the threat and held out his flame ring. The elf was already yelling at him saying we should just run but was drowned out by the roar of flames that shot out from the rings, killing hundreds of carrion rats in a few seconds. More rats kept coming from around the corner, though. Pretty soon Ringmaster realized that if there was a WALL of fire there would be enough rats to extinguish it! Having lost too much time he turned and headed down the halls, the rats' dead brethren consumed moments after having been killed.

Axer occasionally took a few turns too sharp, clipping the corners and grunting in pain, but the sounds made by the rats was distinctive and reminded our cohorts at every turn that a painful death scrabbled down the halls to catch and devour them. The sounds helped them to go as fast as they dared. The blood sucking insects were scarcely given any notice after a little while. We searched and searched for stairs or any kind of opening and finally found a door. There was an indentation in the door and no handle. Ringmaster carefully examined the door and revealed what it's purpose was. "This is an explosive door—if we try to break through it you won't find it difficult." and the monk grabbed Axer's arm as he started in the direction of the door. "No, the difficult part would be surviving the explosion." His face showed both chagrin and annoyance. I let my face emphasize the annoyance. "What's the problem?" I asked them. Funny, right after I said that I had a bad feeling. Almost as if the dungeon itself was saying 'bad idea.' Nigel spun around suddenly, then realized a drop of slime had just plopped onto his shoulder. He swept it off his shoulder and shook the remnants off his gloved hand.

"I'm not sure what you mean—remember that we can't pass through walls like you." Ringmaster said. "Don't you have some contraption you could use to break it from a distance?" I asked him. The sounds of the rats was becoming louder. "That would help if this isn't set to unleash a flamewave through the corridors . . . or something worse. Let's just say it's best to find the key. It should fit into this slot." he motioned to the indentation in the door. "Where's the key?" The elf and I spoke simultaneously. The torch on the wall next to the corner of the hall flickered as the chittering of the rats became more clear. "I would say that it's probably guarded by a minion of Hebbeth's that he would trust not to allow trespassers through."

We all considered for a moment and Ringmaster thought aloud, "It would be nearby, possibly hidden in a chamber. What sort of creature would Hebbeth entrust a key to?" He asked me. I couldn't imagine a creature that Hebbeth would trust. "I don't think he would," I told Ringmaster, piecing it together myself, "He would have to be absolutely sure that the creature would obey. How about a summon . . . a golem perhaps?" I smiled apologetically to them. I was certain the rats would come around the corner any time. Ringmaster shook his head and began moving toward another hallway. "Jordas, you try to absorb some of it's energy to slow it down, I'll hit it with my ice rings to freeze it and then Ferrin will shatter it." We all followed Nigel since we didn't have anything to deal with all the rats. We hadn't gone far when at the end of the long hall we had started down another wave of rats appeared! I hovered above and Slop kept right on going forward—to Slop the rats were the prey. Nigel thought for a second and then unclasped a bulky weapon that appeared to be a crossbow with a metal cylinder on top of it. It occurred to me how absurdly bulky Nigel's armor and items were.

As the two groups of rats came together on either side of us Ferrin (the elf) grabbed Nigel's outstretched arm and Nigel fired his strange weapon toward the ceiling. When fired it sounded like a sword being driven through an anvil and as the clumsy-looking iron spike flew it wobbled and clinked. Connected to it were several small chains. Once the spike anchored in the ceiling, Nigel moved a lever and began winding a mechanism sticking out of the side of it. Slowly the weapon pulled it's way up the chain carrying Nigel with Axer attached to the rope and Ferrin, who was holding onto Nigel's shoulders. The two groups of rats collided and tried to pile on one another to reach closer to the ceiling and get us. Nigel tested his harness and then let go of his strange grappling hook. Pointing his fire ring out, I saw fire begin to form in front of his hand and shouted over at him to stop.

He did and then I floated down and began to absorb what little energy the rats had. Slop kept devouring them, and soon the two groups became one and scrabbled down the hallway we had just come from. Nigel unlocked a lever and he and Ferrin descended to the floor. We waited for a few minutes while Nigel disconnected the chain from the iron spike and dug out an identical spike, attaching it to the end of the chain. He also wound another mechanism on it and when it made a loud clank he announced that he was ready to move again. We went in search of the gore golem and didn't have to look for long. Somehow it must have detected us and came tromping down a side hall. It was halfway to me and suddenly a white and blue ball of electricity flew over my head and crashed into the gore golem. The golem was blown apart by the blast. Nigel and I turned to stare at Ferrin, who was tucking away a wand he had been holding—it was so large I thought it might have once been the head of a magic staff. Ferrin grinned. "I thought you're plan was really good though, Nigel. Truly."

Axer laughed at Nigel outright, "Big smarty man outsmarted by an elf! hahahahaha!"

Other than his eyelids lowering for a moment, Nigel kept an impassive face.

It turned out to be that simple. We took the key, made it back to the doorway without any other problems, inserted it and the door opened, revealing a softly lit room with a pool of beautiful, clear water in it. The pool had a ring of large stone blocks around it that were fit together well and corners of the blocks were rounded. There were even a few stone benches in the comfortably large chamber. Ferrin examined the water, smelled it, and then tasted it. "Fresh, clear water. What is a room like this doing in a dungeon filled with gore golems and demon wraiths?" he wondered. Ferrin gently recited some prayers and poured the pure water down the front of Axer's face. Axer told us he was able to see a little bit after Ferrin had finished. Nigel removed the key from the door and closed it, locking out any rats, wraiths, or vampires that might otherwise wander in. We took turns on watch and rested for the better part of a day. Nigel stayed busy studying the runes carved into the walls all around the chamber when he wasn't checking his items. Ferrin taught Axer a breathing technique and also showed Axer a move designed to cripple an enemy by wounding the nerves in the legs with a precise hand strike. I simply stood around getting paranoid that something was following me.

I spent the time watching everyone else. I didn't really need rest since I still had plenty of energy and hadn't done much of anything. Nigel decided to leave his grappling gun and harness, which surprised us all. Axer's response was immediate: "MINE!" The stupid little goblin hadn't even seen it in use. The monk was trying to comprehend why Nigel would get rid of the item he had either paid much for or spent much time building. We found the answer when he asked Nigel. "There were other options for protection." He paused and pointedly looked at Ferrin. "This nearly us killed it was so slow." Axer, of course, was unpersuaded. He proudly donned the harness and tried firing into the walls to see how effective it was. Not very, but Axer was impressed anyway and quickly learned how to operate the strange machine.

We remained in the chamber, reluctant to leave it until Hebbeth showed up many hours later. As he stepped through his portal, trinkets and charms jangling from his arms and him holding a staff carved from the bone of something massive and ancient in one hand and a wand in the other. He didn't say a word, just advanced, pointing his great, crimson-glowing staff at Ferrin. Nigel had a wand in one hand and a vial of ominous looking steel-blue liquid in the other in an instant. Ferrin raised his hands to begin a defensive spell, but a his face suddenly froze in shocked pain and he stumbled backwards a few steps and fell. He had looked as if he'd been forced backward by incredible pain. Hebbeth was nearly as quick as Nigel, dropping onto his left shoulder and rolling up onto his feet again as the vial of blue substance struck the wall and exploded, sizzling. Shards of dungeon wall and clouds of dust hid everything from view for several seconds. The smoke that came off of it must have been designed to hinder somehow, because as the gas reached Hebbeth one of the rings on his hand glowed bright green, warding it away.

I could sense Hebbeth passed through a wall and tried peeking out to get near enough to him to drain his energy without being blasted by magic. Hebbeth motioned with the hand holding the wand and Nigel's wand was yanked out of his hand and flew over to Hebbeth, who caught it and tucked it into a slot in his belt. Nigel dashed to the side as Hebbeth leveled the bone staff at him and I could just sense the dark magic pulse out of it and dissipate against the wall where Nigel had been standing. The Ringmaster sprinted around the room and covered the floor under Hebbeth in ice. He was so busy concentrating on his target that he slammed into a zombie and both of them were knocked down. Apparently Hebbeth was teleporting his other minions in to assist him against us. I screamed shrilly, hurling myself as fast as I could toward Hebbeth. The necromage turned to me already levelling his staff again and I tried to avoid it.

My formlessness was no help against the magical attack Hebbeth hit me with. Had I been alive my soul would have been blasted out of my body.

Since I was not in a physical body I was merely sent careening through walls for about three hundred feet. I slowed myself for another seventy five and then began heading back to the room where the fighting was. It felt like he had opened a hole in my soul, but souls don't bleed, so I tried to get back as soon as I could. I was almost there when a clawed hand GRABBED me and I felt another pair of hands grasp my ghostly leg. I looked down and saw that a portal had been opened right beneath me and followed me where I went. Demonic entities grasped and clawed at my soul trying to drag me into hell.

Filling myself with my purpose—saving my loved ones and avenging them—I felt a burst of strength from nowhere and flailing, I knocked the claws loose from me. I saw my insubstantial form glowing brightly, and when a demon neared me I heard sizzling and it never touched me. Within moments they stopped bothering me even though the portal was still open beneath me. I reentered the room and saw Nigel struggling to avoid the magic of Hebbeth's staff. The arm that had the fire rings on it was encased in ice, strangely enough. Hebbeth was sidestepping the freezing bolts sent at him by Nigel, so the two were locked onto each other. The Unmarred was also warily stepping around Slop, who kept striking at him, trying to attach to his legs. Ferrin was slowly coming to—he was *VERY* strong spiritually and hadn't been killed by the soul slicing energy. Axer lay unconcious on the floor in the corner, sprawled messily but rousing. I almost reached Hebbeth and he spun and pointed a finger at the floor in front of me, uttering a command word. The place in the floor he had pointed to became impassable. My greatest weapon disabled (draining energy by touch), I began to concentrate on drawing as much energy as I could from Hebbeth at a distance. I wasn't collecting a lot, but it was enough to be significant. As I slowly sapped power from Hebbeth and his magical items, he and Nigel continued their dance of skill, hurling spells and potions at one another with flashes of light and darkness, some sounding like thunder and others silent. Somehow I felt the silent ones were the truly deadly attacks.

Certanius entered the battle. True to his word, he seemed intent on Hebbeth's demise. The axe was spinning like a top—it flew through the air, only a blur. Hebbeth tried to deflect the razor sharp missile but it would flit up, then down and in to slice deeply into his leg. Then up again, then right and then left immediately and in again, like a haste-enchanted dragonfly.

<I have waited long to end your evil, Hebbeth. Prepare yourself for the final blow.> Certanius' axe sawed through the bone staff, cutting it into six pieces while Hebbeth flinched twice and then dropped the pieces he was holding and reached into his armor to take out the wand he had stolen from Nigel. Certanius quickly slashed his arm and shredded the wand to ribbons.

The mage fired two spells of red-glowing energy into the axe and despite how powerful they appeared the axe absorbed them, the dark red tendrils vanishing without a trace. The necromancer concentrated one huge dark orb of power that dissipated when Certanius' axe flew in and slashed off one of his hands. Though he was shocked, Hebbeth never screamed. He just winced and made a dash for his portal. Four steps from the portal there was a 'thunk' and he shrieked and slammed to the floor. Ringmaster had battled the few zombies in the room all into one corner and was turning the walking corpses into charred, sleeping corpses. I don't know if Hebbeth had summoned them or if they had simply wandered into the portal he had opened. Thinking of portals, I glanced down to see the hell-portal beneath me close up. What a relief!

Axer began turning the crank on the grapple gun and the recently mighty necromancer was dragged back into the center of the room, howling in pain all the while. When Hebbeth rolled over and began cursing at Axer, our goblin cried, "BREAKLEGGER!" and struck Hebbeth's leg as Ferrin had taught him, right below the joint of the knee. The mage gasped in incomprehensible pain and fury—and then the axe was there in front of him . . . less than an inch from his throat, the axe spun faster than anything I had even seen. Hebbeth the crippled was breathing heavily, trying to regain his wits. His leg below the knee wobbled as if detached, but with Certanius spinning the axe into a blur right below his chin he seemed to have forgotten about his destroyed leg and missing hand.

"Kill me," Hebbeth warned, "and never escape." The ominous portent of the moment was lost when Certanius decapitated the enemy who he'd both trained years for and given up his body to defeat. Hebbeth's head dropped to the floor and rolled a couple feet, a suprised and pained expression on his face. "Well then, we have plenty of time to figure out how his restraining field works and how to escape this dungeon." I grimaced, annoyed. <Hebbeth did not know how to remove his restraining field. He

has been working on solving the problem for a long time. He had already prepared what he wanted to do: regain control over this land by force using his slaves in this dungeon. I read his thoughts to find out if he had the answer, of course. Why did you think I took so long to finish him?> The axe laid motionless on the floor, the exact opposite of what it had been moments before. The headless body on the floor oozed Hebbeth's lifeblood. Soundlessly, the liquid slid across the stone, bright red conquering the beautiful blue glow the stone in the chamber gave off. The room darkened in a way that involved more than light and shadow.

Axer suddenly became frantic, "We gotta get out of here! We gotta run! The monster's back!" None of us had to ask what monster he was talking about. The giant wraith must have been following us. Reaching out with my senses, I suddenly noticed the foggy darkness that hid it's location from being exactly determined—but it was near. Ferrin was extremely pale even though he didn't appear to have any wounds. He took a stance as if to gain power for another holy spell like the one he had severely wounded the hulking ghoul with before. Only a small bit of magic formed in between his hands when he stopped collecting nearby energy and he considered a moment, then broke off equal parts and sent them into Ringmaster, Axer, and himself to heal them each. After that, he turned to me and raised one hand toward me. I didn't see any magic and had to snort when he said "Be at peace, brother." Somehow I still felt better for the gesture anyway.

Ringmaster and Axer searched Hebbeth's corpse for something that would control the portal. Axer looked up after prying the grapplehook's pointed end out of the body and strolled over to take Certanius' axe in his hands again. He stood next to the body a moment, then told Nigel, "Get back. Axe will find stuff."

He held out the axe and very slowly moved it over the body. Every few seconds the axe would glow a bit brighter and Axer would stop and search that area until he found an item that, when held close to the axe, made it glow brighter. Axer kept glancing at the doorway. When he had scoured the body for magical items we all headed through the portal into Hebbeth's chamber. A crash told us that the wraith was almost in the blue-stone room. "Axer, let's find the key to this portal!", Nigel said. Axer parted with some of the items and they both began clicking anything that could and turning whatever was movable. They had almost finished examining all the items when the Wraith crashed into the room. We could tell because the explosion deafened us for the next two minutes. It began to rise, shaking it's head and then crouched as if to leap toward the portal but it's great head snapped down to the body of Hebbeth—the hound had seen the movement of the prey. The wraith opened it's terrible maw and a stream of energy was pulled from the corpse into it's mouth.

Nigel said "Huh." and he and Ferrin glanced at each other. I wondered aloud, "Hebbeth was still there! Stubborn bastard!" Nobody heard me.

The image of the room through the portal seemed to diminish, growing darker. We could see the wall of Hebbeth's chamber melding with the image of the portal. The wraith finished it's meal, spied us and roared in triumph, then bounded toward the gateway right as it vanished completely. We all listened, not even hearing the roars the monster must surely be making after having it's banquet snatched from it's grasp. Ferrin found a chair and plopped himself down into it with a heavy sigh of relief. Ringmaster found a squat pillar of skulls and scooted it nearer, sitting on it. Axer had Certanius strapped to his back and was holding his pants up, looking for something to tie it at the waist. His pants were so full of things he had stolen from Hebbeth's room that they would fall unless he was holding them. Nigel began to laugh, and I joined in. Axer began as well and we all felt the smile in our mind's eye from Certanius. Ferrin began to snore and we finally quit chuckling and let him rest while we checked the different tomes and trifles in Hebbeth's chamber. As a spectre, I never tired. I would simply get hungrier and hungrier the less energy I had. I was starving.

The intrepid adventurer looked up with a surprised expression and held out a book for my inspection. Neatly labelled diagrams for some sort of complicated machine filled page after page. "That mage was a genius in more than sorcery.", he explained, "He was working out the details of a machine that would cast a spell! This is the first book I've looked at, too."

He shifted a few of the books and then flipped the book he was holding to the last few pages. He looked up again after a few moments, amazement and admiration written plainly on his face. "Hebbeth had finished and fine tuned this design. The last few pages in this book are just notes on ways to improve it. He was adding ideas he thought of later to the machine he'd already planned to build."

The Ringmaster was enthralled by the collection of knowledge in Hebbeth's library. Every half hour or so he'd mutter something to the extent of 'brilliant . . .' regarding the information contained within. Axer was sleeping as soundly as Ferrin before long and Certanius and I were left to talk. <Now that I've completed my mission I don't know what to do. I suppose I could teach my brothers the secrets I've learned in the time I've spent meditating.>, Certanius thought to me. I simply let my thoughts drift back to him in reply. <I thought that once Hebbeth was dead I would be allowed into the celestial kingdom, but everything seems the same as it was.>

Certanius replied immediately, <Revenge isn't as noble as redemption. You got revenge on the mage who harmed you and your family, but doing that doesn't make you better. You will have to search your heart and find out what you need to earn your redemption and then accomplish it. Redemption isn't done in a moment; it takes years, sometimes decades. I've met some who never redeem themselves—not that I feel that you are one of those.>

<Why didn't you tell me that before?!>, My anger clouded the message I was sending Certanius, <You and your idiotic mystery! You're so much better than everyone else you don't have to give truthful answers? So you just make up lies as you go along to trick people into helping you complete your goals! You're no friend at all!> I thought it before I considered everything that I sent to him. What did I expect of Certanius? He was confident in what he had told me before but he had no way of knowing for certain. Suddenly I turned my anger on myself, and at the same moment my hatred flared Certanius telepathically spoke again. <Smother your anger, don't let your hatred control you—I had no way of knowing that Hebbeth's demise wouldn't clear you of your faults . . . . Perhaps it isn't even that at all. You might be meant to fulfill some grand task laid out by the Ancestors above and that's why you're not yet welcome into the Hall Of Destiny. Until you finish your mission you can't return.>

In my heart I sneered (and felt Certanius recoil from me). <You don't have a clue, you're just guessing. I should've known better than to listen to a fool who let his soul be siphoned into a piece of steel.>

No thoughts came from Certanius and when I reached out to talk to him more I found the pathway to his mind like a tunnel ending without a doorway. He was stronger than I was in mind and shut me out as easily as Bonehead could loose an arrow. Nigel turned to me and said, “Certanius is taking the watch if you need to feed.”

Still angry, I threw up my ghostly hands and floated off in search of something to drain energy from. I got an odd feeling, like a supernatural version of being tapped on the shoulder, but when I looked all around me I couldn't figure out what it was. It seemed like something was there—I just couldn't tell what it was.

Hovering through the walls, I slowly circled Hebbeth's chamber, reaching out with my spirit-senses. I could vaguely *feel* the shapes of creatures that were roaming the halls or lurking in some areas. Most couldn't detect me, but a few did sense me. I have survived in this dungeon for years as a wraith while spectres weaker or less intelligent than me have been devoured, dragged into the underworld, or defeated by other creatures or other ghosts. Those that sense me know that I am not easy pickings. Like all of the creatures who are still in this dungeon after so many years, I am a veteran hunter and I am experienced prey.

Down in the dark tunnels of the twisting maze of insanity when you find your way blocked you either give up and let the fingers of madness catch up and enclose you or turn and face the only hunter that is never prey and dash through the palm of madness and out the other side so that you can keep trying.

The first time I consumed a sentient being I had just reached a dead end. I felt my conciousness giving way slowly and saw the ethereal energy keeping my soul on this plane fading. I had been finding what sustenance I could from the tiny animals of the dungeon populace—rats and mice, snakes. Food is scant under the earth. I had been fading away for some time (as many rodents and reptiles as I found, even they did not have enough energy to sustain me) and was contemplating how many insects' spirit energy it would take to keep me on this plane when a kobold—a dumber version of a goblin—turned a corner and found me standing there. It shrieked in alarm and ran away from me. In that moment I felt the thrill of the hunt. When a hound sees a hare bounding into some bushes and it's eyes snap to the meal on legs there's a deeper feeling there. Not just the idea of sating the hunger in your belly. There's something satisfying about being the hunter, tracking your prey and knowing that the prey can't fight back.

I had followed the kobold, immediately catching up to it by passing through a wall. In the back of my mind I was thinking that this must be one of the few kobolds left in the dungeon and how by leaving it alive I might be helping to promote a more steady supply of kobolds in the future. While my mind was considering those aspects, I was quickly closing the gap between the kobold and myself. Suddenly I had found my answer, the way I would survive in this strange new form. I burst through the shadowy hand of insanity, bounded around a corner, and saw another dead end. The hand was back, faster than before and closing more quickly. Nearing the kobold I had almost automatically began to sap away it's energy and felt my essence strengthen. With less energy the kobold's steps slowed and it shouted again in fright and I was emboldened by the hint of exhaustion in it's cry. It's power to resist stolen away, the little kobold slowed further and I fell upon it as ravenously as a vampire on it's prey.

The attack was so much cleaner than all the mess of blood, though. Unlike blood, energy unleashed from a living being slowly floats away, dissipating. As a sentient being that can attract each particle of energy there is very little wasted. Somehow that makes the horror worse. A vampire is a physical being, you can strike it, hurt it. If you have no faith to shield yourself or fight it off (faith as in sense of purpose, willpower) a wraith will sap your body of all energy and leave your ethereal bonds so weak your soul immediately vanishes to wherever the next plane is. There's no mess, no evidence of a struggle or defeat except for the frozen dust that remains of their body—a statue of their last moment frozen in time until something touches it. The slightest vibration sends the dusty remains crumbling into a heap of unrecognizable pieces that shatter into thousands of motes of dust as they strike the ground.

My grace against the hand of madness when I had finished the terrible deed of feeding was my reason. "If I am not on this plane to redeem myself I certainly have no chance of doing so" I reasoned. It was . . . it is . . . my dash through the palm of madness. Without that reason I would curl up in a dead end, gibbering in horror at what I'd become. My reason was hope for myself—faith that a larger idea was at work behind my existence, a scene I wasn't yet able to view. Anyone who says they don't have faith is an arrogant fool. How can we hope to know the reason for everything?

A bunch of strong beacons of energy loomed up in my senses and I also felt the drumbeats and heard the eerie music that hadn't been able to penetrate the thick, safe walls of Hebbeth's chamber. I was sensing a different type of creature that I hadn't felt before, but they had large stores of energy. Large sentient beings near the middle of a dungeon? I didn't recall hearing of anything like that before. When I moved close enough to make out the vague shapes they appeared close to humanoid but with long snouts and they had large tails as well. When I got close enough to sense that they were reptilian one of them turned and stared at the wall of the room he was standing in—looking in my direction.

Chapter 4

Cold Blooded

Although I could tell one of them would have enough energy to replenish me I didn't take the chance of facing them. We are all veteran hunters in this dark place. More energy not only meant more food—it meant more willpower. Enough to gather all that energy and contain it. It also meant a greater chance of spellcasting, and although as a wraith I can drain energy I can still have my energy blasted away by magical means. It frightened me that the nearest one had sensed me through the wall as well. I found a mighty giant vampire bat and drained it of all energy, then returned to the chamber where my allies were. "There are many great chambers not far from this one with many . . .", I wasn't sure what they would be called, so I used the best words I could to describe them, "Lizardmen."

Nigel recognized it immediately and marked the page in the book he had been reading, sitting back in the chair and raising his eyebrows in thought and acknowledgement of the reputation of these lizardmen. "What is their history?" I asked him. Suddenly I had that stupid feeling again, like someone was there waving at me and I couldn't see them. "Do any of you feel that?" I blurted out. They all glanced at one another and seemed to purposefully ignore my question. A few akward moments passed in silence.

"Well," he started hesitantly, "I'm not sure what to tell you about them. They are similar to humans, but tend toward their darker natures. They are renowned both for their prowess in combat and their magic. I think that most adventurers who plan on meeting up with them overestimate their spellcasting ability because most adventurers aren't used to fighting a mage. As long as we stay well away from them I think we'll be fine, though. I'm more worried about what we're going to do to get out of here."

With that, he unstopped his flask and took a couple long swallows, then considered a moment before plugging the cork back in. "I've skimmed through several of these tomes and haven't found any way we can leave this dungeon. Portal spells are absorbed, so you can't even send a portal to the other side of the boundary. Something was bothering me about that. "It seems like something would be possible using a portal spell. I know the gem that maintains the field can absorb a lot but it must have a limit." I told him. The ringmaster just shook his head and put his fingers together, popping his knuckles. "It expends energy to improve the invisible wall once it has an overabundance, so the only way I can think of that we could overload it is to try to build some of these designs he has for spellcasting machines—From what information I can find out about the blocking field I don't believe that will succeed, though." He looked past me to several diagrams of various demons and other creatures that could be summoned. The pages were held against the wall by some grotesque faces who's mouths were able to be opened by pulling down a tiny lever on the top of the ugly heads and would snap shut again once released.

Nigel rose and more closely examined some of the pictures, particularly interested in a sheet of parchment emphasizing the importance of magical wards to protect one's senses from succubi. Yes, the ideas for protecting oneself from being hypnotized were quite instructive. Being dead I was able to concentrate on reading the print. Nigel studied the pictures longer. No doubt he was considering the best way to combat them physically. Heh heh, sure. Anyone who summoned *any* demon, not just succubi, better be prepared to control them somehow. I always hear about demons that try to beguile you with deals or charms, but in the end a demon comes down to claws and teeth in my experience. The object isn't to convert you into a demon, it's to destroy your body. Once that part is done, they use the same tactic of brute force to *drag* your soul into hell. The best of us have strong spirits and lots of friends, and therefore usually not much to worry about from demons. The average person is far from the best of us, however.

Take heed, evildoers: When you meet your end you'll miss the people you made into enemies. Some of them may even help to pull you down!

Suddenly I was hit by a crazy idea. "Is it possible to reverse a summoning gate?" I asked Nigel. He turned and raised an eyebrow, then furrowed his brow and frowned a moment, looking at the floor. His expression changed to one of thoughtfulness and then he looked at me with eyebrows raised. "It would take some calculations and a little bit of knowledge about summoning gates, but if you can pull something out you should be able to put something in.", He said. Grinning, he added, "Of course, the being-in-hell part would be tricky."

He began sifting through the papers and half-finished charms and potions on the desk, then spied the neatly ordered bookcase and glanced at the mess on the table once more, disgusted. He grinned at me and then strolled over and started checking the titles. "Someone would have to summon you from hell once you were there. Of course they'd have to be *outside* the crystal's force field, and I haven't the slightest idea how to attract someone to the edge of the dungeon when we can't leave it. You certainly wouldn't want to stay in hell for very long, I'm certain of that! In fact, it would be a much better idea if the summon portal was ready before you ventured into the underworld."

<I could attract someone's attention>, Certanius thought to us. "What reason does anyone have to help us once they have been brought to the edge of the crystal field, though?" I asked them. <Do you have any family or friends outside?>

Nigel nodded right away, "Yes, I have many friends and some people even consider me a hero. I'm sure someone would be pleased to receive the renown of rescuing Ringmaster the Dungeon Trekker, savior of Prince Aldrenni and-"

<Give it a rest>

"Give it a rest"

The savior of Prince Aldrenni narrowed his eyes, but stopped. Clearing his throat he reiterated, "I'm well known." I never asked where Prince Aldrenni was Prince of.

He pulled out a book labelled 'Summoning Circles And Other Useful Equipment' and it turned out to be what we were looking for. It explained . . . in **GREAT** detail, the process of making different summoning circles. In the early days of summoning apparently they were summoning squares.

In fact the author of the book had a lot to say about summoning squares. The general idea was that squares were better than circles. In fact they are better in every way than circles. IN FACT, if you use circles you are a MORON. I decided he was quite mad regardless of how well put his argument was. He was obsessed with the fact that it made no sense to use circles when squares were more effective and listed many reasons, some that made sense and others that used assumptions that leaped from a reasonable train of thought into some outlandish principle he had come up with.

Whatever the case, he had all the basic principles covered and many advanced theories and developed ideas as well. Nigel found some blank parchment and an ink well but began yawning after he searched for a pen for several minutes. Annoyed, but more tired than angry, set the book and the paper on the table with the ink well next to it and dug in his pack and unrolled a small blanket just big enough for him to stretch out on. He was snoring in ten minutes.

Certanius and I didn't speak with each other for the next five or six hours. There is a point beyond boredom where you are just numb. It's the closest I ever get to sleep. Literally I stood, dead to the world for hours upon hours, unthinking. Other than getting that strange feeling again a couple of times.

A knock at the door startled us all. Then Certanius startled us telepathically, <Lizardman at the door, he regularly reports to Hebbeth on the progress of the army's training. They are becoming skilled more quickly than expected. The Elder Dragon, Sissoks, demands to know how long it will be before Hebbeth is ready to attack.>

Slop was crawling up the wall near the door, preparing to drop onto the lizardman if he entered. First knocking to gain attention, then impatiently banging on the door, the lizardman finally began slamming the door as hard as he could and shouting, "HEBBETH! OPEN THE DOOR! Sissoks DEMANDS TO KNOW YOUR PROGRESS!"

I'm certain the messenger heard the others shuffling around. They were taking positions and preparing for a fight when sounds of cursing began to come through the door. We heard a keyring and the lock's bolt turned.

The lizard took one look inside and leapt backward as the chain of the sharp end of the grappling gun's chain flew toward him. A small bolt Nigel loosed from a miniature crossbow also missed the lizardman by inches. No sooner had the projectiles passed above him than he rolled to the side of the door frame. I floated into the doorway as we heard a sword unsheathed and when the lizardman spun around the doorway he literally sidestepped right into me. Immediately I drank deeply of his energy stores and his next footstep didn't make it past his other foot. I wouldn't say he stumbled and fell. I would say he force-fed himself stone from the way his mouth, open in surprise, cracked against the floor.

I could barely remember what teeth feel like and I winced, too.

A few stabs later, we had a fresh lizardman corpse. I got a feeling like someone was watching me and turned around to scan the dungeon. I had a faint notion something was there. Like a ghost's shadow. When you become a free-floating spirit you become more sensitive to a sixth sense. It's more like a gut feeling than a sound or a touch. Someone was trying to get my attention, and it was someone familiar to me, but so low on energy that even I could hardly detect them. Intently I tried to focus on the area that most felt like the source, but it was still difficult to know if it was just my paranoia or something actually there. It was time to put an end to this little game. "Alright, I want to know if you are all feeling what I am." Ferrin was helping Nigel push desks in front of the door and stack the heaviest books they could find on it, but he replied, "For quite a while."

Nigel responded with a nod and I felt Certanius answer telepathically, <I can tell it's a sentient being, but I can't track exactly where it is. It moves slowly because I've lost it during our more hectic moments, but it has caught up to us each time we stop.>

A paper rustled loudly and floated to the floor, attracting everyone's attention. Axer grabbed the page and threw it over his shoulder with a shrug. Nigel walked over and rolled his eyes as he passed Axer, who had already turned his attention to polishing the grapple-launcher. We gathered around Nigel to see the message the ominous parchment held. It was a diagram of different bones in the skull that could be used in rituals or spells. "Bonehead!" I said at once. It was starting to make sense. When his bony form was crushed into a fine powder and no spirit was evident in the vicinity I had assumed Bonehead had simply passed on to the next realm. Here was proof that he was actually trying to contact us and come back!

We all began looking around through the books and papers for some spell or incantantion that would allow us to bring our ally into physical existence. Ferrin found the spell we would ultimately decide was the best: the ritual of return. After Nigel examined it he said, "Something seems wrong about this. I can't put my finger on what it is, but I am certain of it."

Despite his worries, he finally conceded that it still appeared to be our best shot. The ritual of return needed a corpse to lock the spirit of the target into the physical world. The lizardman had provided just what we needed as well as if it had been planned. We began preparing the ritual by finding all the ingredients. There were so many bottles containing powders and potions of almost anything. While we were gathering the ingredients, Nigel found several jars and vials he packed away for later use. When everything was ready, we applied the salves and mixtures to the corpse and put it in sitting position, drawing the appropriate symbols to aid in the revival. The rest of us backed away and watched as Ferrin protected himself with enchantments moved forward to complete the ritual by calling out the name of our companion three times and touching a candle to the body. I would have jumped along with Ferrin and Nigel if I'd not seen the buildup of energy and the soul fly into the body before the eyes widened and it flinched.

He began to blink and look around at us and suddenly there was another soul leaping into the body! As the body convulsed, another spirit fought it's way into the body. The convulsions became more and more dire and Ferrin screamed, "What did we do wrong?!"

I had watched as we followed every step to the letter as closely as possible. suddenly there was a snap from behind us and we turned to see what it was, but all we saw was an open vial flying toward the body. Ferrin's reflexes were amazing—he was reaching to catch the vial, but he was a quarter of a second too slow. The vial busted on the body and the shaking stopped, the eyes closing tightly as if he were trying to withstand more pain than his body could contain. His mouth was open in a silent scream for a few moments, but suddenly THREE voices burst forth!

The pain seemed to subside after that and one eye opened, then the other. There was no mistaking it as we looked at each other—we had each heard THREE voices. The lizardman's body slowly seemed to come under control, but limbs moved independently of one another, and for a minute the body on the ground simply writhed around uselessly. As the motions began to correspond with one another the body rose. "We're back." three voices said in unison.

Who? I wondered.

—

Sissoks slowly opened one eye. One of his lizardmen stood before him, about the same size as Sissoks' eye. Sissoks, though annoyed at having been woken, waited patiently. These short-lived beings couldn't stand silence for long. "Master, we still haven't been able to halt the beast and Felltower hasn't reported back with Hebbeth yet. It . . . withstands any attack. We have even tried fire."

Sissoks opened his other eye and rose, although he could only crawl in this dungeon. "You have tried false fire,", the ancient dragon's information was almost a growl, "True fire will destroy this rodent." The lizardman kneeled. Now he was going to beg for help. Sissoks scowled even before the general began to ask, and spoke the word of true fire. 'Please' melted into a howl of surprise that lasted only a second. Sissoks listened for a moment until he pinpointed the battle and crawled toward it. Sissoks felt rock press in close, but his scales were stronger than stone and scraped away anything that would have impeded a lesser being. An old dragon, his scales had been scratched so much that the color was more gray than green.

The beast was an energy drinker, but it wouldn't matter. As Sissoks entered the chamber that served as the largest yard for the city of lizardmen, he growled in anger. The sound broke spears of stone loose from the ceiling and they shattered when they struck the ground or dragon's scales. A third of the city had been decimated. The ghoul sensed the enormous well of energy Sissoks possessed and loped toward him. The master of the lizardmen opened his maw and uttered the word for true fire. It was magic, but it wasn't. The word for true fire was a part of every dragon's spirit. Even with true fire, the wretched wraith plowed forward for eight seconds, nearly making it halfway to the mighty dragon. When the resistance of the wraith ended, it's body was turned to ash instantly. The moment the body disappeared, a dark shockwave emanated forth from the disgustingly evil creature, the foulness of the cursed death destroying and cursing everything nearby. It left thirty of Sissoks bravest lizardmen lumps of gory tar and hundreds of others fell down weeping with the intensity of the curse. Sissoks felt the blast of the shockwave stab into his soul, and he gasped in torment as a single tear fell from his left eye. When it hit the ground, flames shot forth from the spot and a hole burned straight through the rock out of sight, a teardrop falling straight to hell.

There was a rumble as lava slowly seeped forth from the hole. Sissoks roared in anguish for the first time in ages. His howl of pain and rage levelled most of the remaining structures in the lizardman city. When his voice's echoes died away, he looked at his claws and saw that the color of his scales had deepened to black. Just as before, the marks of his lifetime, the gray scratches, were there. Sissoks felt his body's vitality had been sapped away, and he unleashed his fury with true fire at the ceiling of the cavern.

White fire burst forth and burned through the rock, sections of superheated stone sloughing down like the red rain of hell.

On the surface, a small town was rocked by a huge explosion as four houses were blown to pieces by a blaze that erupted from the surface. For an entire minute the cry of the dragon went on.

In the ruins of the city, Sissoks gathered his people around him. "WE WILL FIND HEBBETH!" He commanded. "HIS SUFFERING SHALL NOT BE MATCHED!" he decreed. His people cried out in agreement, passing out weapons. "AS THE SUFFERING OF HIS PEOPLE SHALL NOT BE MATCHED! THE TIME OF THE OTHER RACES HAS ENDED!" The lizardmen roared their master's name, and Sissoks knew that his name would be known as the word of destruction.

—

It took some time before the possessed body made sounds that were recognizable as speech after that. The first to speak said, "You are all great fools to interupt my plans. As you can see, death is not the last word when one is wise in magic. You have, however, cost me time and forced me to replan my rise to power. You will pay in suffering, I assure you." The possessed raised the right hand and a dark spell glowed at it's end for a second, but it began to fade and the scowl on the face twitched and was suddenly replaced by a smile. <That was Hebbeth. We've undone our own work.> Certanius informed us angrily.

The next thing the possessed said was, "You called me?"

<Bonehead.>, Certanius confirmed. The possessed came to each of our companions, extending a hand in greeting. "You've always called me Bonehead since it took me so long to say anything." To myself and slop he gave a cursory nod. "I don't remember my birth name, but I'd rather be known by another name. One that isn't an insult."

To that I nodded, considering names. One seemed much like the other. "What about Martin?" I asked, but by his mild smile I could tell it would be perfectly alright. "Excellent. Thank you.", he replied. "I need to test my skills in this body." He told everyone. For a moment his hands were a blur in the air before him. He still had the ability to make certain movements at an incredible rate of speed. "Splendid!", "He said, "Yet our new friend has been waiting for his turn patiently. I'll be inside." He waved one hand in the air cheerfully and then the hand dropped and the features changed on the body. It had been difficult to tell before, but as the muscles repositioned, it became apparent that when Hebbeth and then Martin had control their expressions were much different than the lizardman's.

<Felltower, the lizardman we killed.> Certanius identified the being before us. After a long pause, Ferrin mumbled, "Well, this is akward." Felltower examined our group for a few moments before addressing us, "Sissoks awaits my return with an answer from Hebbeth. Being together in the same body, we share most thoughts, and I have seen that the wizard is more treacherous than expected. It was his intent to enslave all of our people with his demon magic." For a moment, the expressions on the face shifted into a malevolent scowl and magic began to form around the body, but as suddenly as it had changed the energy dispersed and Felltower's appearance returned to normal. "Even now Hebbeth wishes to continue his plan, so I ask that you break this body so that he cannot carry out his corrupt dream."

None of us had expected for Hebbeth to be waiting and for the ritual of return to allow him passage into the body we had called Martin back to. Ferrin told us, "There are priests and mages with greater powers than ours that I have seen perform great things. Somewhere, perhaps one of the larger cities where I travelled through, there may be one who can seperate the spirits." Nigel agreed, "After all we've been through bringing Hebbeth out with us to justice shouldn't be too hard. Think of the payoff as well. There are rewards everywhere for his capture." Personally I could care less about the reward, I just wanted to free my family and friends and see Hebbeth destroyed. "I think it's fine to bring Hebbeth to justice, but I want to remind you all I have people to free from this dungeon. I've only been through a small part of these lower levels and I could find and save them a lot faster with your help.", I told our group.

Martin spoke up, "Felltower and I are in agreement that Hebbeth should be captured and together we can suppress Hebbeth without a problem, so we will help to find your people and free them. How many are we seeking?"

Thinking back on who I remembered from my village, I was surprised that I could only think of eight. The thought filled me with guilt for forgetting the others, but perhaps we would cross paths with others while seeking those I remembered. "my mother and father, My friends Harvey, Amelia, and Stanley, and Arthur and Gerald, who were shopkeeps. There were others but after all this time I can't remember their names." There were a couple names I remembered that I didn't mention. A pair of troublemakers with bad intentions, they could rot here for all I cared. As we gathered what we needed for the reverse-summoning gate, it was strange. I got the odd feeling we were being watched. I couldn't tell if the others felt it, too. Once we had what we needed we started out, following the left wall of the dungeon so we could scour the lower levels for the people I was trying to find.

Nigel's boots had begun to lose their glow, but he dug in a pocket and got two small tokens out that had holes poked out of the middles and untied his boots, feeding the bootlace through the hole before tying it back up on each boot. Within a half minute the boots were glowing brighter than ever, and we turned left at the first intersection. The hall we followed, as most of the tunnels in the dungeon, was wide enough for five people to walk shoulder-to-shoulder and broke into many passages in every direction. Following our plan, we of course turned down the very first left-hand opening, which was big enough for two people to walk shoulder to shoulder. It began to stink badly and it seemed to grow darker and wetter the further we went.

Nigel stopped after a short time and told us, "I know this passage doesn't lead anywhere, let's go back." Ferrin gave him a quizzical look, asking, "How did you come to that conclusion?" Nigel just shook his head and began backtracking, gruffly responding, "It doesn't matter, the light is going this way. Come on." Noone really cared, it seemed the tunnel wasn't really occupied and we had seen no signs of movement, so we would simply try the next path. Halfway back to the entrance, Axer slipped and fell. His suprised cry turned to an angry grumbling and he got back to his feet and adjusted the straps of the grapple gun he carried. "Stupid rock!" he growled, giving the inanimate object a swift kick.

The entire tunnel growled back. Nigel shouted, "We're in a mouth!" and began running as fast as he could with his huge backpack toward the entrance. Everyone slid off their feet as the entire tunnel—that is to say, the throat of the creature—moved backward. Nigel activated his fire rings and began burning the roof of the creature's gullet with flames. It stopped moving backward and simply writhed in pain. It's howls were deafening and the shifting caused great difficulty in moving without falling down, but Nigel kept releasing small blasts of fire and we finally reached the edge of the tunnel. The creature that had inhabitated the tunnel slid backward into the darkness, retreating from the fiery attacks.

"It didn't like the taste of that." I observed. Everyone laughed, glad to be OUTSIDE of a mouth. We continued searching caverns, some as still as the grave, others chittering and pattering with life. Very few things troubled us. We avoided one hallway which was carved with crude designs because we could hear goblin voices shouting and chanting. We didn't need to fight an army of goblins. It was slow going as we searched for my undead family and friends, and Ferrin shared some of the knowledge he had gained from decades of study. "Souls who are at peace," Ferrin told me, "Have no reason to stay in this world. They move on to the next world."

Axer kicked a rock down the hall, drawing everyone's attention for a moment. Ferrin sighed and shook his head, turning back toward the path. Nigel hissed at him, "Keep it down, you little fool! Did you not learn your lesson in the tunnel-worm's mouth? Quit kicking things!"'

"But I'm bored!" Axer complained loudly. "There aint any people down here! Let's get out of here!"

As it often happens, a negative attitude turned out to be just what we needed. I sensed a prescence while Axer continued complaining about his sore feet and the smelly elf. I began to turn toward them even before they spoke. "Jordas?" A dark shape stepped from the shadows. Before my years in the dungeon, I would have been horrified to see the being before me. I recognized the features of my friend, Harvey, in that broken body. I was confused for a moment by the movements. The body resembled a zombie, but the movements were smoother and had purpose. A reanimated corpse, a zombie, will only follow the directives it is given. If that shell of a person has a spirit, it moves differently. A regular soulless corpse moves as if it's limbs are pulled by a puppeteer's strings, but a spirit directs the body in a much more natural manner.

"Jordas, it's been so many years. I thought I was damned to walk these terrible corridors forever!" The blood-stained face still bothered me, and I could see the blow that had ended his life was similar to mine, a wound from a greatsword had torn away his right arm, and his face showed a deep gash apparently caused by the tip of the sword since the slash was in line to touch the point at which his shoulder had been cut away. "Harvey, my friend! How great it is to see you! That damned sorcerer, Hebbeth trapped you as well, I see. We'll make the bastard pay, but it's so great to finally see a familiar face! You've survived in this awful place!" my happiness was about to give in to despair, though.

Harvey's face was contorted in a mix of pain and pleasure. "I cannot cry!" he choked on his anguish, "When I couldn't even cry I knew," his voice broke with bitterness, "I knew that he had taken everything!" Everyone was quiet for a moment—even Axer.

Harvey's face rose from his hands and he clenched his fists. Bones in his hands popped loudly. His face was a visage of hate, lines of anguish, determination, and fury creasing his face. "I swore I'd repay the torment he imposed on me and I will. Oh, I will fill his body with the pain of ten thousand tortured souls—and when he begs me to end the pain I will laugh! Ha HA HAAA! My revenge will be complete and I'll go on torturing him until the angels themselves urge me to stop! I will make him suffer until he dies of madness!" Harvey's laugh was never grim and sadistic until now. As Harvey's rant continued I knew that Hebbeth had not only been responsible for his demise. The imprisonment in unlife Hebbeth had forced onto Harvey had destroyed his mind and was working at his soul, too.

The possessed were violently shaking, and I assumed the other two were preventing Hebbeth from doing something stupid. I snapped Harvey out of his insane babbling, "Harvey! Harvey! My friend! HARVEY!" He stopped what he was saying and looked straight into my eyes with confusion. I reached out to him one more time, "It's going to be alright now. We'll get the others and make it out of here."

I knew from the way Harvey's face changed that there would be no happy ending. "I don't want to get out of here. I'm going to make that bloody necromancer pay . . . pay! PAY! PAY! And what about the others? Others? There aren't any others. There aren't? I've searched every cavern. Yes he went too far when I took my tears. The others? They would want the same. REVENGE! 'REVENGE!', they'd shout! AVENGE OUR FATHERS! AVENGE THE SISTERS! AVENGE THE CHILDREN! AVENGE US ALL! REVENGE! ETERNAL TORMENT FOR THIS NECROMANCER!"

Suddenly Harvey was whispering, "It's all that's left. You can't save the others. There aren't any others. REVENGE! You can do THAT! Make this necromancer pay!PAY!PAY!PAY! He's even taken my tears. Nothing left . . . nothing left but REVENGE! Nothing left . . ." Harvey trailed off and stared right through me. I moved and his eyes didn't follow me. Revenge was all that Harvey had left. I found that I wanted to cry at that point, too. We could kill Hebbeth, but his spirit would remain free. Better that he should suffer than to simply haunt this realm for centuries. Nothing Harvey could do would be enough torment for Hebbeth, and I knew what would happen if Harvey learned that Hebbeth was one of the three spirits possessing the body of the lizardman—I wasn't willing to put Martin through that even if the lizardman was the scum of the earth.

I turned to Ferrin and asked, "Do you have enough energy to free him?" and Ferrin nodded sadly. The possessed stopped shaking suddenly. There was a determined look on the lizardman's face. Ferrin began to form an orb of holy energy which produced light and the feeling of warmth even though I was a shade. There was something wrong with the feeling though. As if it were letting you know you don't belong here—I would definitely feel more than warmth if it touched me. I backed away. Harvey's eyes were fixed on the glowing ball of light. Until the possessed suddenly hunched slightly and a sneer replaced the determined look. Nigel leaped at the lizardman and Ferrin put the finishing touches on the energy. Hebbeth sidestepped the big adventurer, who crashed to the floor, and spoke to Harvey, "I used your sister for months. She was never very good, but your sons made fine garments."

Harvey's eyes snapped to Hebbeth . . .

. . . and Ferrin flung the holy energy into the zombified Harvey. The light flashed and the energy sizzled the body into ashes. Harvey's mouth was open in a soundless scream and above the sizzling was the sound of hell's own whirlwind. Hebbeth opened the mouth of the lizardman in some depraved spell and we were all slightly pulled toward him. As the last remnants of Harvey's body burned to nothing, there was red energy hanging in the air where he had stood. It was a frozen image of Harvey's last moment and my first impression of it being the final particles of his body being vaporized soon was replaced with understanding. Hebbeth was sucking in EVIL energy from the moment of ultimate loss he had just inflicted on Harvey.

Hebbeth finished absorbing the energy and his booming laughter was a stain on all creation, a triumph for monsters and demons everywhere, and a slap to the face of the Great Spirit. It was the most horrible thing I have ever heard.

Chapter 5

Punishment

The most horrible thing I have ever heard was the best thing to happen to Hebbeth, though. The lizardman body had a dark red aura that . . . seeped and oozed and burned like a flame that was melting as it poured out of the body. I wasn't sure how Hebbeth had overpowered both Martin and Felltower, but if he could push them aside and take control at a moment like that one, I didn't think the other two had much of a chance of controlling the body now that Hebbeth was supercharged. Without a word, Hebbeth extended both arms out, clawed fingers outstretched toward our monk and red electricity leapt out to bite into our ally.

Ferrin seemed to be stunned except for reacting each time another jagged bolt tore into him. Nigel was rushing at Hebbeth's back with a sword out and Axer fired the grapple gun through me at the Hebbeth. I could tell by the sorcerer's motions he was already preparing for the goblin's attack, though. He seemed to pass the energy jumping from one hand to his other and as the grappling spike flew towards him he used the empty hand to bat the projectile aside. He moves resembled the earlier actions I had seen Nigel perform with his rings and magic wands and vials; they were well-practiced and connected fluidly.

Hebbeth, Nigel, and even Ferrin were on a different level of combat than most of the enemies I had seen. Nigel didn't just grab a wand and use it on you, he was already moving to accomplish his next task and was planning the next four or five. The same was true of the elf's martial arts. I had heard elves were naturally graceful, but it seemed magnified when I saw Ferrin unleash a flurry of punches or a combination. Every motion had another motion it could be connected to. Hebbeth was reflecting the same mentality in battle. Nigel skidded to a halt before running into Hebbeth and in what I will call *heightened concern* promptly backpedaled and threw a vial at the mage's back. Ferrin slowly fell to his knees, still being repeatedly stabbed by the red lightning bolts.

Hebbeth turned and caught the vial in his free hand and smiled cruelly as he shook the hand holding the vial once, as if flicking water at Nigel. Ferrin took a few more hits and fell forward into unconciousness. the moment the elf's face slapped the floor Hebbeth raised his other hand and closed it in a gesture of containment. Nigel shouted in pain and seemed to be trying to get something off of himself, though no danger other than Hebbeth was apparent. Smugly, Hebbeth turned to Axer and tossed the vial up into the air above the goblin so that it would fall near the little pest. Axer countered Hebbeth's vain maneuver by dropping the grapple gun and turning to dive and catch the vial. Not the smartest move, but unexpected. As Axer got to his feet and held the vial in front of himself he chortled in his gravelly goblin voice, "You sure throw bad!".

Not the smartest taunt, but effective. Hebbeth frowned. Then he snorted and raised his hand to pummel the nuisance with some sort of magic spell and found that he had three problems. One was that he rapidly losing his supercharge because I was draining away all of his energy. The second was that his arm stopped responding to his command to unleash his attack thanks to Martin and Felltower intervening. The third problem was, as with most of our enemies, was that he forgot about our slime. Slop struck from above (it's usual tactic) and Hebbeth was immediately blinded, in pain, and suffocating. Suddenly he stopped struggling and stood up straight, arms at his sides. Slop was suddenly jerked entirely off of his head and flung into a corner. I felt a powerful will encompass me like a bubble and it moved me away from the wizard into the same corner as Slop. He opened his eyes, narrowed them at me, and his hand stretched out, it's shadow rising from the floor to cover his hand. Then it began to expand as Hebbeth approached me. I was about to pass through the wall through the wall behind me to escape and approach from another angle when he stopped walking. the shadow-hand vanished and his arm abruptly went to his side.

Nigel stopped struggling with his invisible (Spiders? Snakes? Evil faerie bitches?) attackers and went over to help Ferrin, but made certain to face the lizardman at all times. His face was pale. Axer had pocketed the vial and picked up the grapple gun again. Curious as always, he asked me, "Did you eat his brain?" to which my obvious response was . . . actually I told him I did. heh, heh. He got a wide-eyed look and backed away from me and then set to polishing his grapple gun. He kept a wary eye on me, though. Axer would be immune to my brain-eating attack.

Certanius explained <I penetrated his mental defenses while he was concentrating on fighting. I managed to disable him, and it should prevent him from regaining control for at least an hour.> Axer nodded, "Good teamwork! Break his skull then eat his brain!" We all chuckled. Axer didn't get the joke, but chuckled with us.

Felltower had taken over his body and made a slow circuit of the room after letting us know that he and Martin had done their best to stop Hebbeth from taking control, but Hebbeth had withdrawn from them and pushed himself forward with a burst of stored energy, taking over for just long enough to hurt Harvey in the worst way possible right before my friend was forced out of the material realm. The terrible evil he committed caused Harvey's spirit to overflow with hatred, horror, and anger. Hebbeth had sucked in that energy and used it in his assault immediately following. He had used a large portion of that energy to retain control of the body. It was only when Martin and Felltower worked together that they stopped him from using a spell at Axer.

We had already spent a lot of time searching for those I wanted to try to track down and help, and I had a lot more worries now than I had before we found Harvey. If the others weren't here as he had said, we were wasting time. The longer we spent down here the greater the chance Hebbeth would find a way to attack us again. Nigel had unfolded his bedroll and pulled it along with Ferrin laying on it. The red lightning had severely wounded him. Fortunately he was conscious and seemed to be thinking clearly, so he would be alright eventually. I had to hope that the souls of my dearest family were at rest. I couldn't face them if they were gibbering with insanity. I couldn't face anything if I found my mother or father crazed by the horrors in this dungeon.

I stopped and the others halted as well when they saw that I wasn't moving. "Guys," I told them, "I don't think I want to find any of the others that I knew. If they were as mad as Harvey was, I couldn't stand it." I had no idea what I would do. There was a silence and then Ferrin asked, "If you aren't going to search for your loved ones any more, why aren't you at peace?"

I felt the reason deep within. Down in the center of myself I felt a chill deeper than any ice as I realized why I was staying in the material realm. Instead of retreating from my fear, I reached out and accepted the reason. "Until Hebbeth has received his just punishment, I will remain."

The shadowy hand of madness engulfed me, but it could no longer harm me. I understood my motive and realized there was nothing to fear about it. I had not lost my mind. It was perfectly reasonable that I would stay and ensure that Hebbeth faced the consequences of his terrible actions. The others didn't know my heart, so I'm sure that they felt the cold shiver that hinted I might become like Harvey. They couldn't know my heart, though. I hoped they would choose to trust me.

We moved much faster when we concentrated on exiting the dungeon. We avoided all the various problems we had faced when scouring every room. Like many of the older stories suggested, Hebbeth's dungeon would periodically change it's layout by way of shifting walls. You never actually witness it unless your travelling undetected through the dungeon because the spells were set up to avoid someone seeing the change take place. A goblin in a homemade suit of armor challenged Axer to a fight in order to win the grapple gun. The challenger won the fight, but not before Axer struck him in the leg with the technique learned from Ferrin. As the challenger limped away, his leg twisting grotesquely with every step, I marvelled at how stupid goblins were. He won the fight, so he got a cumbersome grapple gun and a busted knee. Other than the gun, Axer only had a bloody lip to show for the fight. Yet the punch had cost Axer his grappling gun.

"Come on," Ferrin said, "You fought well, and it's not like you goblins have that much honor to lose. Axer growled at Ferrin and mumbled something that didn't sound like 'thanks for putting that in perspective for me'. We continued upward and Axer kept grumbling and kicking rocks and stomping on bugs until Nigel spun around and shouted, "ALRIGHT!

OKAY, AXER! I need you to STOP doing that so that I can think and hear clearly! HERE!" and then Nigel dug into his pockets looking for something shiny or mechanical that wasn't important enough to withold from the goblin. After several items went back from whence they came, Nigel slung off his pack and rummaged through it. Axer edged closer and closer and tried to peek into the backpack. Nigel looked up and smiled at Axer (who was practically drooling all over himself by this point) and thrust a hand out with a small item in his palm.

Axer's eyes widened and he snatched it out of Nigel's hand and slipped it onto a finger. The silver ring had crimson flowers carved into it and a cluster of tiny gems in the center of it. Nigel took Axer's hand and touched the gems in the center of the ring to the wall. "To activate the ability you have to picture a red rose." The well-versed adventurer told our goblin. Axer closed his eyes for a moment and then looked at the ring frowned. Nigel just smiled and told him, "Move your hand away from the wall."

When Axer did an image of a chunk of wall exactly like the one the ring had just been touched to hovered above the ring. "WOAH!" Axer cried, waving his hand around and watching the illusionary copy of the wall stay aligned with the gems in the ring.

Nigel was pleased with his solution for about ten minutes as we continued. Unfortunately Axer was now required to touch the ring to everything. It wasn't as bad as kicking things and stomping bugs, but the tapping we heard every twenty seconds was pretty disruptive, too. Nigel marched ever onward, working hard not to show his annoyance. Ferrin was trying to hide his smile to avoid rubbing in Nigel's mistake. The air continued to grow less humid as we got closer to the top floor of the hellhole. Although we had dealt with far worse adversaries it seemed that we were spending more time fending off the weaker, less intelligent enemies we ran across. Big spiders (giant, but not **HUGE**) and other large insects were some of the more common ones.

There were a few skeletons that didn't have the intelligence to avoid battling us and, of course, some zombies. One zombie surprised us by grabbing Nigel's throat from behind and pulling him backward. It was about to take a bite out of his throat, too, but Nigel had a trick none of us had known about—he slapped his left leg and there was a loud click.

Just as the zombie's teeth began to clamp down, Nigel slid a hidden blade out and jabbed it in the exact center of it's face. It was buried almost to the hilt and the zombie kept pushing it's head forward to get closer to Nigel's neck, but he had a good grip on his sword and held it's head there while our body-sharing comrades stepped over and put some torque on the zombie's neck, tearing it's head off. The lizardman's face smiled and Felltower said, "I've never felt so powerful! This shared strength is excellent!" and the face slightly changed to a big grin and Martin said, "It feels so good to feel my muscles and skin again . . . well, scales anyway . . ."

The dungeon continued to grow brighter as we neared the outer area of the uppermost level. At any moment I expected to see the light of day for the first time in years.

Then we turned a corner and saw a dim light shining at the end of a tunnel.

Between us and the light was another group of adventurers, though. One who had a headband marked in it's center with an eye closed her eyes and held her hands out toward us. I began to move sideways, wary of magical attacks, but she didn't send out any magic missiles. Instead she opened her eyes and pointed to the lizardman. Then she ominously declared, "Hebbeth is hidden away inside this body". The adventurers she had with her immediately drew weapons, taking stances and preparing spells.

Nigel, Ferrin, Martin, Felltower, Axer, and I all shouted for them to stop, to wait, to give us a chance to explain, that we weren't on Hebbeth's side, and that they'd better not be stupid. I couldn't even hear myself in the ruckus, but while we tried to convince them not to attack us two of them shouted battlecries, magic began to tingle and spark on the air, and then a large group of vampires attacked both of our parties.

By "a large group", I mean thirty of them. I know vampirism spreads quickly, but I didn't have time to contemplate how so large a group stayed fed in this part of the dungeon. It became obvious right away that these vampires were suicidally ravenous. A lightning bolt tore through the air and one of the vampires exploded into ashes. There was a suction of air for a moment and then a burst of wind picked another vampire off the floor and spun him in a horizontal cartwheel into the group of frenzied bloodsuckers. Slop was burning one up, Ferrin got to his feet and a holy bolt slammed perfectly into the chest of a fourth undead berserker. With a smoking hole where his dead heart used to be housed, the vampire slowed, stumbled, and crashed to the ground, finished.

I stuck close to one and it howled and hissed and roared in frustration, but it didn't matter. With no willpower left, it had no defense against me. Particles of it's body began to flutter away as all sustenance remaining in the body was stolen. In a few seconds it was incapacitated and I left it there to latch onto another one that was circling Ferrin. The monk had impressive holy energy which burned them each time they tried to grab him for a clean bite, so they were looking for openings to slash or strike him in the hope they could weaken him enough to attack with their preferred weapon . . . their fangs.

The other party's warriors were buffeting the onslaught of vampires and rapidly dispatching them with well placed sword strikes (right through their hearts). I could tell they had a good formation. This group had practiced and planned thoroughly for battle. We were really tearing the vampires up when I heard roaring laughter. The vampire I was draining crumpled into a heap and I moved to another one, while seeking out the source of the laughter. Nigel was laughing triumphantly as he unleashed all of his anti-vampire equipment. A vest covered in stakes. A pump that sprayed clouds of garlic juice. Gems that lit up almost as bright as the Sun. I noticed there were several crosses stitched into the clothing he wore. Nigel was a vampire hunter. Despite all the spells and mighty skills of war possessed by the others fighting the vampires, Nigel easily dispatched twice as many as any of the other adventurers.

Of course, there was one vampire who outlived the others. The vampire lord moved much faster than his subjects, and they were very fast. The vampire lord was also much STRONGER, though. Ferrin, who was already weakened from the other vampires' attacks, was yanked backwards off his feet. The combined groups turned to help the priest but he had been hauled down the corridor a hundred feet and the vampire lord was already gulping blood from his neck.

Nigel was running toward them and suddenly a large vial was in his hand. Instead of popping the cork, he held it in one hand and punched the vial with his other hand. After he'd done this he flipped droplets from his hand at the vampire lord. We were able to tell when the first droplets touched the vampire master because he hissed and recoiled, his eyes glowing red pools of hatred. Nigel brought a sword around and came in close for the kill and suddenly the sword was sliding across the floor and the vampire lord laughed and pulled Nigel's head aside to go for his throat!

We were rushing toward Nigel and heard a loud 'thunk'. At the same time, spikes suddenly protruded from Nigels arms, legs, and back. One of the Swordsmen in the other party had already put up his sword and was checking the other vampire corpses for valuable items, but he stopped at the sound and then chuckled, clapping. "Nice!", he complimented Nigel's anti-vampire armament.

Despite the many stakes that had impaled him, the vampire lord slumped against the wall and took a long time to die. Nigel messed with some levers and a crank on his armor and rewound the stakes back inside his thick armor. I looked over the gathering and noticed that the possessed were missing. Looking over to where the looter was, I noticed that the possessed had been caught by some sort of magic net and was laying on the ground with a look that was equal parts chagrin and annoyance.

They had two people workin on Ferrin and Nigel handed one of them another vial he had packed away. Both of the healers looked wide-eyed at the vial and then at each other. The elder of the two took the vial and applied it to Ferrin's neck as the younger one with tattooes worked healing spells over him. Everyone else was shocked when Ferrin sat up a minute later, blinking and seeming to be fully restored. The female in their group turned a man who had a very nicely crafted bow and said, "This is the time to capture the necromancer."

The man just nodded and put up his bow. He called to the youngest of the group, a boy who could not have been older than thirteen. The boy had been watching the healers and they had been explaining something to him about the liquid in the vial that Nigel had given them. The elder of the two healers nodded in appreciation to Nigel and handed the empty vial back.

The female, obviously a sorceress, stopped in her tracks and made a slow scan of the room. I had felt it, too. The same mysterious prescence that had been following us since the whole ordeal had begun. The Old man who had put up his bow snapped his fingers and the sorceress blinked and turned back to the possessed. "Hold on, that body has more than one soul in it!" I told them. The man dismissed me with a wave of his hand, the old fart. He and the sorceress stood back and began weaving some very strong spells over the possessed body. The spell went on for nearly two minutes and then they stopped making different gestures and stood still. The old man snapped his fingers urgently and the youngster cautiously approached and held a big yellow gem out. He slowed more the closer he got to the field emanating from the possessed. As he reached the edge of the field a bolt of lightning flashed between the gem and Felltower's body. It happened again and I was afraid the old man hadn't listened to what I said, but he suddenly dropped his arms. The sorceress gaped at him and when he didn't continue to assist her, she dropped her arms as well.

"SIMON! Hebbeth is still in the body!" She pointed. Simon turned around to her, confused that she didn't understand. He began to say something and then Hebbeth began to chortle. Everyone was on guard even though he was trapped in the magic net. Hebbeth began to gloat on how he was going to make us suffer but Simon slammed Hebbeth into the wall with an outstretched arm, stunning him for a moment. In the silence Simon explained, "The other souls are not our worry. We just needed to seperate Hebbeth from them in order to contain him and set the others free." As we all got the joke we began to laugh. Hebbeth was a very powerful necromancer and had spent much of his time building his spiritual energy in order to cast spells, unlike Martin or Felltower. Simon had placed his trust in that Hebbeth would understand the spell he and the sorceress were casting and would try to maintain his hold on the body while the others were sucked into the gem, so instead of an epic struggle to pull Hebbeth into the gem, he simply yanked the others out and left Hebbeth. Hebbeth's magical might was his downfall, and he had been so focused on a mental and magical fight to control the body that he had been easily outsmarted.

Simon had the healers (when Ferrin didn't step forward Simon motioned him to help out as well) stand ready and told one of the swordsmen, "You will take out the heart and the healers will repair the body." The one he had ordered to take the heart was the same one who had been clapping earlier when Nigel's trick had defeated the vampire lord, and he didn't even glance at Simon. "What, he stole your heart? I keep telling you, you have to give love time to grow. You didn't think to bring your formula for cutting out evil necromancer hearts? Wait a minute—The old codger told us earlier that he didn't like Hebbeth, didn't he? Stand back! Hebbeth has bewitched our beloved Simon!" The fighter held out an arm to back everyone away and confronted Hebbeth, "You vile incubus! Stop using your immoral charms on him or I'll cut out your—oh. Isn't that funny?" He leaned against a wall and smiled at Simon, who only narrowed his eyes and turned to a platemail-clad warrior who was already moving forward. "I'll do it. Heaven forbid our unflinching hero should have to soil his soft hands and innocent heart on so terrible a task as capturing an evil necromancer." The warrior brought out a black-bladed dagger and told Hebbeth, "You may want to brace yourself. This may take a while."

Hebbeth spit right in his face and he staggered backwards and made a disgusted sound, wiping it off his face. The comptemptuous fighter leaning against the wall laughed, "What sorcery is this?! Put down your visor! Protect your eyes from the terrible demon venom!"

The warrior gave the fighter a withering look and looked at the others. Rolling his eyes, he put the faceplate down and moved in to do what needed to be done. The elder healer explained exactly how it would be handled. The warrior hadn't lied, it did take a while. In fact, he had to stop to rest. Hebbeth was pinned to the floor the entire time by magic spells held up by Simon and the sorceress. The youngster was also helping the mages, much to my surprise. Hebbeth threatened, howled in fury, threatened some more, and then only screamed. After a short time he didn't even scream any more.

A complex spell involving switching the souls in the two containers (the heart and the gem) took place once removal of the heart was complete. Simon pronounced it finished and then the heart went back in the body and the topaz was placed into a rune-covered box that snapped shut and locked. Felltower stood again after being healed and stretched. Both he and Martin verified that the process had been correctly completed. As one group, we travelled toward the sunlight at the end of the last tunnel. The closer we came the more brightly it shined. It had been so long since I was at the wall of the dungeon I didn't even remember feeling the sunlight. It supercharged me—I didn't have to feed on anything, because I had all the energy I needed. It felt like I had been breathing the stench of an outhouse through one nostril for years and suddenly I was taking huge breaths of fresh, CLEAN morning air.

I knew I had to make sure Hebbeth was punished, but the sunlight was so beautiful that I was ready to leave him and the physical world behind. Just a little further, I told myself. Soon it will be over.

Felltower was the first to realize that we were past the point the indestructable field should have been.

As the others joked and laughed, I heard Simon say, "That was easy.", and wondered where the hell that old man had been that made fighting a huge group of vampires easy. I looked down at Slop and said, "We're free. Free, Slop!" I was ecstatic, but I was still dead.

"Stop, everyone, stop." I told them. Everyone looked at me and quieted down so I could speak. I tried to think of something lasting I could leave them with. "The road is long. If things get too difficult call on me and I will help you. You have proved your prowess in combat against the vampires and you seem genuine enough in your purpose. What I ask of you is easy since you are already taking that path, but I want to charge you with it anyway. Make sure Hebbeth faces justice. It is what those of us who have suffered at his hands deserve—it is what we need."

I turned to Nigel and Ferrin and told them, "You are my friends. I hate to leave you with the burden, but the light of day has cleansed my soul and I am going home. May you be blessed forever for your true hearts and hard work." After I had said that I patted Axer's head and Certanius and I mind-linked for a moment to share a farewell. Axer asked me to tell a goblin named 'wheelhead' that he was sorry. "I will, Axer, I will.", I assured him.

To those I had recently met I said, "I don't know you very well, but your actions provide enough proof that I trust you with the same task." All of them made some gesture of respect or farewell . . . except the fighter with the big mouth, who just said, "I charge you not to make any more speeches." The tattooed guy next to him punched his shoulder and he looked at the tattooed healer and then back at me and said, "No, really, I mean it."

The big warrior snorted and rolled his eyes and I felt a gentle tug from another place. “Make sure you finish it.” I said to them one last time. The sunlight became blinding as I felt myself moving in a direction I didn’t know existed. Only Certanius responded when I tried to say goodbye to them. <Goodbye, friend>

—

I felt myself reattaching to the physical world and slowly my vision faded in from a blinding white light to the soft colors of dusk. I knew I’d been someplace else and was only now returning and I knew that something was wrong. Everything else in between the final farewell and my return was blank. The white tube of light that shielded me pulled away back into the sky and suddenly my senses returned. I was alone and vulnerable again. All the warmth quickly fled as I stood there staring into the sky, wishing I was still . . . wherever I was before. All I could remember was a soothing peace. I heard a commotion further down the path and turned to see what it was. The entire group hurrying down the road stopped with shocked looks on their faces.

“Jordas?” A young man in tattered white clothes asked with a bewildered face. Memories rushed forward. The assault on the village, the necromancer’s trap, the years of feeding off of the energy of other living beings, finding allies in the dark maze, and then the crescendo as they hunted down the necromancer and stopped his terrible plans. I realized I was naked and covered myself, then realized I had a body made of flesh and blood! The group gathered around me and offered up some clothing, which I used immediately. It felt like there was a chunk of ice in my belly as they all greeted me meekly. As my memories settled, I closed my eyes as if pained and bowed my head. “You lost Hebbeth.”, I knew at once. They were too ashamed to say anything for a few seconds. Finally I asked, “How?”

The sorceress responded as soon as the words were out of my mouth, “He has a familiar. It stole the gem and we have been chasing it back to the dungeon. It’s been pulling away from us every step of the way, so we need to hurry before it finds a way to restore Hebbeth.” We all started moving and I enjoyed the cool breeze on my face as I pieced together part of the puzzle. We had not found the Ritual of Return by accident or hard work. The familiar had placed it in a convenient area for us to find when otherwise it would have taken weeks. All that time it was following us and

I had felt it, even under all the layers of enchantments. Simply put, I had forgotten about it. The night creatures were prowling around and some bats passed overhead as the sun left the sky to the moon and stars.

"I should have used a different spell." She said as we neared the entrance to the dungeon. I knew the effect of regret too well to avoid reassuring her. "You did the best you could, I'm certain.", I said. The others echoed agreement, even the fighter they had who was usually sarcastic. Simon, who our new allies seemed to look upon with respect and awe, even went so far as to tell her, "When we have more free time I'd like you to teach me how you casted the fireball so quickly." She was speechless, but the others were still praising her talents. Nigel and Ferrin both agreed that they had never seen someone react so quickly, much less cast a spell in that short a time. The boy who seemed to be learning from all of them told her, "I hope I can be half so skilled someday." He smiled approval and she blushed from all the compliments. Soon her inability to stop the imp would be forgotten thanks to our companions. If the members of our group were as genuine as they appeared to be then I wanted to keep the lady focused on the task at hand and not punishing herself over some mistake she made. Especially if it wasn't a mistake!

Before entering the dungeon I explained to Slop that we needed it to test the forcewall of the dungeon. The wall's mysterious absence was a boon, but we didn't know if that was only a temporary reprieve or if somehow the wall had been taken down permanently. Slop never communicated, but after I asked it to check for the wall of energy it slurped inside and disappeared into darkness. A short time later it came back out. We looked at each other and as Simon and Nigel started for the entrance the smartmouth came from behind and stopped them. Beckoning with one hand while the other blocked the two experienced adventurers, he motioned the sorceress to proceed. Nigel made a face instead of saying, "Idiot.", and Simon looked apalled that the man would dare cross his path. Rolling her eyes, she went ahead. The jester looked around at them all and feigned angry innocence, "Some people just have no respect for honor and integrity these days!" I both couldn't tell and didn't care whether it was a joke.

We went about ten steps into the pitch black before someone bumped into a wall. Nigel's glowing boots hardly lit anything. The big cleric with the tatooes called to another ally, "Elwin, does it feel evil in here to you?"

and the other healer they had told him, "Beyond a doubt—but we can take care of that!" I could feel the power emanating from them, and two glowing orbs of light pushed the darkness away from us and held it outside a circle of twenty feet from us. Another orb of light pulsed to life and I saw that Ferrin was helping to push the radiance outward further. We were ready to go now and yet another small orb of holy energy lit from the boy in our group. Felltower and Martin stayed just outside of the sphere of holy energy so they didn't get banished. Axer looked like he was a happy as ever and had his mouth open in wonder and glee watching the orbs give off the soft, pleasant light. We made our way through the next few tunnels and then heard goblins screaming in the distance. The pitter patter of little feet was unmistakeable as the goblins approached. We heard a shout of terror followed by a sound like rocks crumbling. The sarcastic fighter sounded annoyed as he told Simon, "I didn't take this job to get buried alive. We should get out of here and create an earthquake to just bury him in this damn dungeon!"

Simon just shook his head and asked, "Clay, you don't even have the slightest idea how much magic it takes to make an earthquake." and the sorceress pitched in, "You also have to have the strength to stop it unless you don't care about the consequences." Clay turned to her and sneered, "How does being buried alive complete your mission?" There was no answer for that as the goblins came running through the big dark chamber we were in. As they saw us they screeched in terror—in the goblin mind I suppose they were thinking they had no allies and had just run into a trap. Not even one of them tried to attack us even though Simon picked off one with an arrow and Clay slashed one who was running past. It squeaked and crumpled into a heap. The one with the arrow in it's belly laid there screaming until Clay stepped over and finished it off. It was unnerving that even goblins wouldn't defend themselves they were so scared of something.

Ferrin, Elwin, and the other two holding glowing white orbs of holy energy brought them together and pushed them into one ball of light that lit the entire center of the massive chamber. There was a muffled yell as a goblin came staggering out of the adjoining chamber, but it looked like he was covered in gray goo. He continued going slower and slower, taking each step as if slogging through mud, until he finally stopped moving. He appeared to be a statue of a goblin now. Nigel gasped, "No! It's an Oculus! move back!" Everyone took Nigel's advice and began stepping back. The orb of light was left in the center of the room. Simon had an arrow notched and a spell was ready in the hands of the female spellcaster. Swords were drawn and one was handed to me. A floating, gigantic head came into the edge of the light. It was covered with small tentacles that had eyeballs at the ends of them. It's face had many eyes and also had a mouth that opened as the Oculus saw us. A screech came from the Oculus that made me want to cover my ears and I saw that the thing had row after row of pointed teeth. The illusion that the goblin had been turned to stone was broken when the Oculus suddenly flew forward and bit off the upper three-quarters of the goblin. The sound of stone being shattered was as unmistakeable as the sight of fresh blood spraying out of the doomed goblin's body.

With another ear-piercing shriek, the Oculus charged Clay, who stood out in front. Simon hit the floating head in the side with the arrow he had notched and Clay spun counter-clockwise while stepping to the right of the ugly monster. When Clay finished spinning, four of the tentacles on the Oculus' left side fell to the floor, gray goo seeping out of them. Every scream the Oculus made was an attack of it's own. Clay covered his ears and retreated from it and he wasn't alone. The Oculus narrowed all of it's eyes in fury and then it span in place. The gray goo that turned things to stone flew everywhere just like a dog shaking off wet fur. It didn't cover anyone, but some of it did get on each one of us. Not only did the goo make it more difficult to move, it also stung the skin and had a strong smell that stung my nose, mouth, and eyes. It stopped spinning, shrieked again, and then flew at high speed through the air toward Simon. The old man dropped his bow and held out both hands and a distortion filled the space in front of him. When the Oculus hit the distortion there was a loud thump and it went spinning away. At the same time, Simon got knocked onto his butt and the distortion vanished.

"A sight for sore eyes." Clay said as he stomped on the eyeball-tentacles he had lopped off. The Oculus spun to face us again and screeched again. When it did I noticed that our sorceress and the young boy were both starting spells and the screech dissipated the formed energy as they covered their ears. The Oculus picked out the nearest one of us, which was still Clay, and opened that deadly maw as it flew at him. As it came on, Clay suddenly fell over. We all realized at the same instant that Clay's foot had been stuck to the ground when he stepped on the tentacle-eyes. The berserk monster slowed and swooped down to take a fatal bite from the fallen fighter's midsection. The young boy was there suddenly—he must've pulled a sword and dashed in right after his spellcasting was interupted! The boy stabbed downward into the open mouth and we all covered our ears as it screamed in pain twice more. The giant head had recoiled when it was stabbed, and the boy had fallen on his stomach, losing the grip on his blade. Clay gave the boy his own sword and the boy fervently hacked at the stone connecting Clay's boot to the floor. I took note that Clay had an arm over his eyes so that he couldn't see the boy swinging the sword so close to his leg.

Another arrow punched into the Oculus from Simon's bow, and then a barrage of sharp ice shards pummelled it from our sorceress. The Oculus shook and spun until the blade wiggled free and fell to the floor, then it screamed and spun again, throwing more of the crippling gray goo everywhere. We were all struggling through the hindrance and tripping over chunks of the hardened substance everywhere. The other fighter, the possessed and I strode forward together to take it down with swords. The Oculus stopped spinning and saw us boxing it in, so it flew out of reach above us and screeched again. Simon's next arrow missed as the Oculus moved just out of the way. Our sorceress threw more ice shards at the thing and instead of avoiding the stream of tiny missiles it flew into them and straight at her. When she realized that the Oculus was about to chomp down on her, she stopped sending little frozen knives and dived to the side. The Oculus veered to try to catch her, but missed.

Axer threw Certanius, who began to spin very quickly and home in on the Oculus. We were running toward the monster's position when Certanius cut deeply into it in two spots. After the second cut, however, the axe fell to the floor of the chamber mostly covered in gray goo.

I heard a 'woosh' of air and half of a quiver of arrows stabbed into the side of the Oculus. It unleashed another one of those terrible screams, then slowly lowered to the ground before screeching again, but this time it didn't sound like you were having knitting needles stuck into your ears. The monstrous head made a pitiful sound and fell forward, dead as stone. Within seconds it looked like a strange rock. "I'm thinking that the plan Hebbeth and his familiar have is to slow us down until they can formulate a new plan,", I told the others, "and it's working." I demonstrated by attempting to move my left arm close to my body and failing. "Yeah, that's for certain.", Nigel told me, "Wow, I'm surprised that we were able to beat an Oculus that easily!", he complimented everyone.

The boy and Clay looked at each other and then back at Nigel and the boy said, "THAT was EASY?!"

Chapter 6

The Obstacle

Nigel just nodded seriously and explained, "There have been armies felled by only a few of these, if you read your history. Although this is the only one I've ever actually seen."

"Poor goblin." Axer said, looking at the two goblin feet that were still attached to the ground. The warrior who hadn't spoken very much patted Axer's shoulder and reminded him, "If he didn't get eaten, he would have suffocated in that stone covering.", and Axer thought about it for a minute and then nodded and smiled, "Lucky goblin!".

Everyone shuddered and Clay said, "Now I know what you mean when you tell me 'good luck'. I don't appreciate that." to the big warrior, who just smiled brightly. Nigel had a vial that dissolved stone, but he used the entire thing and some of us still had splotches of stone on us. The majority of the liquid had to be used to free Certanius from his stone prison. Clay's sword was permanently sheathed in stone with only the point showing. Clay removed most of the stuff in his backpack so that he could carry the sword with him anyway. "I paid far too much to just abandon this weapon here," he said, "especially if there is something that can get the stone off of it."

Nigel was holding a finger and thumb at the top of his nose as if pained and he informed Clay, "Those were gorgon's tears, and they cost more than . . ." Nigel calculated for a few seconds and said, "More than half of the other equipment I carry with me. The price goes up every time I look for more."

Clay grinned and said, "I have something right here that would make a gorgon cry!" and I couldn't help but chuckle. "Wanna see it, Michelle? You can tell me how much it would make you cry!" Clay asked the sorceress, who smiled sweetly and said, "It makes you cry enough for both of us. Although . . .", she paused, "I would pay for a vial of *your* tears."

Clay started to say, "How much would you pay for a vial of-" when Elwin cut in with, "SO we should probably go the direction that the—was it called an Oculus? That the Oculus came from to reach Hebbeth, right?" It seemed to be correct, so we continued in that direction, Ferrin and the tatooed cleric picking up the orb of light to bring it along. As we kept moving, Clay and Michelle kept up with their remarks until it was all we could do to keep from giggling at everything they said. The big tatooed cleric asked the young boy if he thought that Michelle and Clay would make a good couple and Elwin heard him say it and reprimanded him, "Drake, I think their sarcastic attitude is something that young William here would be better without." Drake put up his hands defensively, "Easy there, High Priest. It doesn't hurt to have a bit of humor."

"I'm serious, Drake, I'm sick of you mocking me that way. I just don't want the next generation to grow up jaded and sharp-tongued. There are enough problems in the world already." Elwin responded. Drake's hands drooped and he held them out in a gesture of exasperation as he said, "I wasn't mocking you!" and then Elwin went on about Drake called him 'High Priest' when he knew very well that Elwin was currently only a acolyte of the order and that he should have more respect for the High Priest than to use the name in a joke. It wasn't long before I found myself talking with Simon and the other warrior, whose name was Vincent, about battles that had happened back before I was killed. Vincent was the veteran of six wars and, although he had aged better, was nearly as old as Simon was. Apparently Vincent had survived some very grim situations and recovered from wounds that most died from. Simon's approach to war was that instead of seeing each battle it was more important to organize the location of your fights so that a general would have the greater advantage in resources above everything else.

Vincent and I agreed that while resources were very important, there were other factors that took precedence. Vince gave Simon an example: "I've been in a battle where we were outnumbered and many had told us we were wrong, but with two fine captains and a superior will to succeed branching from them, we took the fight to them and beat them on their own ground."

When he finished, Simon snorted, "Superior will to succeed? I remember hearing about that battle. The Few Against The Many, right? You won the fight, but they torched all the food stores and in the end you had to retreat! I admit, it makes a much more inspiring story without that, but fact and inspiration don't usually coincide."

Vince looked appalled, "We broke the main force of an enemy four times our size! The point wasn't to take their food stores, it was to show that one of our men was worth four of theirs! The whole fight wasn't about destroying the evil Tharanians, it was about crushing the foe's spirit so they wouldn't *want* to fight us any more."

Certanius joined in as well and as we spoke on the subject and Clay and Michelle continued with their back-and-forth, Axer began singing a goblin marching song and beating two rocks together that he had picked up.

"You can't count on the element of surprise for every battle!" Vince angrily shook his head, and Simon opened his mouth but was interupted by a calm, deep voice none of us had heard before. It said, "The element of surprise can win a battle outright, however, so it's certainly not to be underestimated." Axer kept banging rocks and Clay and Michelle kept laughing at one another, but those of us conversing about the tactics of combat froze.

A line of black barbs appeared in the side of Simon's neck and he winced as the breath went out of him and he crumpled. Vince turned and shouted in alarm, hopping backward as a claw as big as his midsection dug tiny furrows into his breastplate. The possessed and I turned at the same time that Williams and Nigel did and we all gasped.

As I looked at the Manticore, one of it's paws flipped out in a blur and I felt four snakes slither across my chest. The Manticore leapt over my head and I looked down at my bare chest not comprehending what had just happened. Strips of my ruined shirt laid on the ground before me and there were four wide white marks across my body. Understanding came as the pain struck me and the white marks began to fill with blood. As carefully as I could, I knelt and laid down. Looking out to try to take my mind off of the hurting, I sought out the strange, stealthy monster. Unlike the Oculus, which was an enraged beast, the Manticore was a true monster. The head of a old man who had a very long beard and no pupils in his eyes looked out and spoke as the winged lion's body leapt from here to there over our heads and the tail with it's many barbs swung threateningly back and forth.

It padded toward Michelle, who conjured up a ball of fire and from it began to spout a stream of flames. The old man spoke a few arcane words and the fire went out of it as if a great breath of air had swept it out. Michelle shouted in pain and alarm and backed away, her hands blistered from the fire. The Manticore picked up it's pace and Clay tried a slash from it's rear flank, but the tail swept out and nearly struck him in the face. Vincent charged straight into the Manticore and met it's attack with an attack of his own. The claw knocked him down and then recoiled from the sting of his blade, but the face of the old man never even turned toward him. It stated, "Bravery allows one to face a lion. Stupidity causes bravery to be seen as a mistake."

With that the Manticore hopped onto Vincent's breastplate and the warrior began to pull a knife, but he locked eyes with the empty spheres in the old man's face and he froze. As the Manticore had jumped onto his breastplate, the tail had bumped into Michelle's stomach, and she fell backwards with quills jutting out of her stomach. The young boy hurled a swirling blue sphere of energy at the Manticore and it leapt over the blue ball and landed in front of William saying, "The advice of the ancient may be wasted on the young, yet as much the efforts of the young may be wasted on the ancient." Those were the Manticore's final words as Slop dropped from the ceiling of the cavern to land over the old man's face. The sound the Manticore made was nothing like a human scream. It was the reverberation of hell-spawned fury and the futility of a hundred lives wasted for no reason.

I rolled over trying to put the pain of the gashes in my chest aside, knowing that the Manticore's cunning might surpass our ability if we didn't take advantage of every oppurtunity. The paws were quickly rolling Slop together to remove it all at once. Ferrin and Elwin were trying to stop the nasty work of the poison in each barb that had struck Simon and Michelle, but Drake had unfolded a Scythe and strode toward the Manticore with grim determination. Axer called his long winded battle cry, "BE AFRAID, OLD MAN! NOW YOU FACE AXER, WHO STOLE THE MAGIC AXE AND SLAYED THE GIANT WIZARD! THE AXER THAT SURVIVED THE THOUSANDS DEATH RATS AND BROKE THE NECROMANCER'S LEG!", then charged at the Manticore howling like a berserker. I was a step behind Axer as the goblin swung Certanius and added another sentence to his title. I swung full force at the back leg of the Manticore and definitely struck true. The sound of metal slicing into bone is impossible to forget. It's tail had been Axer's target, and in another slash he completely severed it. The monster spun and threw Slop right into my face. Even though slime wasn't actively trying to eat me that was little consolation as it covered my arms and small droplets spattered into my face. In seconds Slop was off of me, but as the air touched my arms the agony in my chest was forgotten for a moment.

The Manticore turned toward Drake, who swept out with his scythe, murdering the air where the Manticore was a moment before. Before it landed on him he had time to say, "Oh-".

As it's claw reared back to rearrange his features, Clay jabbed his dagger to the hilt in the back of the arm that was raised. A wing swooped down and smacked the top of Clay's helmet, sending him reeling. When he was struck, he made a sound between 'narf' and 'oofngth'. If you can pronounce 'narfoofngth' I'd say you could empathize with how Clay felt, I'm certain. As Clay tried to reorient himself, The Possessed punched the monster's side so hard that we all heard ribs crack. With incredible speed, the Possessed began punching the side of the Manticore. The bone-crunching sounds began to sound like someone punching pudding after three seconds of the rapid punches that signified that Martin must be controlling the body. The Manticore's body backpedaled defensively, but the bloody face of the old man still showed no anger. The face was passive, as if no pain nor emotion was felt. Drake was back on his feet in no time at all and the Manticore pumped out the rear leg I had cut and kicked Axer down. The monster was now near the entryway of the chamber, the doorway we had come through. Axer got back up and together he, Slop, Martin, Drake, Vincent, and Clay all approached it.

Having wounded it multiple times, we had the advantage, but the Manticore backed down the hall as they approached and blue and white electricity began to flash in front of the old man's face. Nigel glanced up and shouted, "BALL LIGHTNING!" louder than I'd heard him shout anything before. Axer lowered his weapon and said, "Oooo!", while The possessed continued to advance and the humans dived away from the opening. Slop raised up as if it was a snake about to strike and the ball lightning grew larger for a quarter second before impacting on the slimy menace. Jagged tendrils of electricity electrocuted the Possessed and Axer. As Slop was electrocuted, spiky protrusions erupted from it and and then jiggled. The voices of Martin and Felltower were each distinct and Axer's voice was a wavering, repeatedly interupted 'woahwoahwoahowowowowow'. Nigel sounded certain when he said, "Well, that's it for Slop. I don't think Axer will survive, either.", and then he turned back to helping Ferrin with Simon. Michelle was sitting up looking dazed, and Elwin was gently shaking her and telling her to focus. William picked up Simon's remaining quiver of arrows and his bow. "Get out of the way!" he shouted to those blocking his shot in the hall. Electricity still leaped from one spot on Slop to another, and the slime bubbled. Axer said, "Woooah." and stayed in standing position as he toppled backwards. The Possessed bolted forward and jumped onto the back of the Manticore.

The Manticore was no animal ready to shake and rage if someone grabbed onto it's back. It jumped straight up and impacted the top of the tunnel. When it landed, we saw one hand of the lizardman's body begin bashing the top of the old man's skull. The Manticore shook mildly, then crouched and slammed into the ceiling of the corridor again. When it landed the second time, William loosed and struck the center of the old man's face with an arrow. When the fist of the Possessed crashed down on the old man's skull again, blood and gray matter squashed out of the front of the face as it split. The Manticore didn't flail around in death. In a deliberate motion the body lowered itself down and put the ugly remains of the head down as if resting. The wings carefully folded back down and it 'went to sleep'.

"That," I said, shivering, "Was very weird." Nigel looked at the positioning of the Manticore and smiled apologetically. "Yes," he said, "Demons have many different forms, and some have more . . . unnerving tendencies. Seems like it's ready to get back up at any moment, doesn't it?", the Ringmaster chuckled nervously. My chest was itching terribly and I remembered that my arms weren't nearly as badly harmed as the engraving the Manticore had practiced on my body. Now the front of me was covered in blood, and I felt the room spinning. The last thing I said before I blacked out was, "I hope that spinning is just me."

My eyes opened and I looked out over the world. All of it. Black and White intertwined so closely that almost everything seemed gray. I saw a soldier in a suit of gray armor and his heart was shining white. His opponent, another soldier in gray plate, ran toward him with a shining heart of his own. As they closed the distance to one another, Their hearts flared brightly and began to dim. Gray swords bounced blows off each other and the soldiers' hearts darkened with each blow. More soldiers began appearing from opposite sides and fighting with one another. One of the first soldiers breached his enemy's guard and planted his sword into the foe's chest. The gray heart vanished and the victorious soldier's heart was pitch black. As the same process repeated with random victors on both sides, the first victorious soldier watched them fight for a short time and then examined himself. He had become a shadow. He dropped to his knees and wept shining tears over the corpse of his enemy. Slowly, a spark lit inside him and his heart shined again. The soldier stood, realizing his mistake, and rushed to a pair of fighting soldiers. He pleaded with them to stop, and shining tears fell from his gray face. The soldiers stopped fighting and looked at him. They listened, then they pointed to their hearts, which were dark, and faced each other again. The victor raised his sword high as the victim slowly sagged and fell. It wasn't long before the winner was on his knees, shining tears running down his face.

Some of the winners didn't stop and look around. Their forms grew larger and more terrible to behold as they stalked the battlefield, butchering weaker soldiers. One of the repentant soldiers stopped and met a shadow warrior and raised his hands in surrender. The shadow soldier cocked his head sideways, not understanding what the brightly lit figure was saying. After a short time, the dark warrior looked down at his hands and jumped, shocked. The shining man put his hands on the shoulders of the stalker and seemed pleased, but the dark-hearted soldier shook his head. A single tear, bright as a star, rolled down the cheek of the featureless face of the dangerous form. Raising the brutal serrated and spiked sword, he brought it down on the shining figure, who flashed brightly and disappeared. The stalker stood there contemplating what had happened, then looked at his hands again. The process repeated more often as the fight continued, and then suddenly there were no more soldiers joining the gray sides with their meaningless banners, only heartless silhouettes standing around looking at their hands. When nothing remained except them, great bars rose and enclosed them all. The gray background split open and revealed a congregation of shining people with a blinding light behind them. To the side stood the gray soldiers who had been slain before becoming a bright singer or dark slayer and the shadow warriors in the cage saluted those outside the cage and drew their weapons, facing off against one another. The gray people were ushered through a doorway as the silhouettes began killing each other. Whenever one of them fell, however, he rose after a brief period and began fighting again. It wasn't sad or horrible at all, the dark figures seemed as pleased as those outside the cage. Those outside the cage built magnificent structures and sang and danced.

The visions I saw continued and I didn't grow tired of them although I felt like I watched for a long time. On the other side of the cage, behind the dancing figures and the beautiful buildings, I felt the contentment of the blinding light. Eventually I grew curious about the gray figures who had exited the scene, and my view shifted to a gray world with two gray armies. As the battle lines charged each other, I saw their shining hearts flare and begin to dim as their blades met. The cycle continued closely resembling the previous vision. When the cage appeared over the new shadow men it grew as the first shadow warriors entered the prison. Outside, shining souls entered through the gates of the fantastic, endless city, and then they joined the first bright spirits. There were still some gray men standing aside, and after seeing the city and the cage they were ushered out. This time I kept watching the dark figures. There was still grief there, still anger and hostility and pain, but somehow they were satisfied. I laughed in wonderment at their manuevers and the techniques and felt the determination they had. This was not ugly, it was just a different sort of dance.

Looking past the cage, I wept when I viewed the city of dancing figures. Some came to the bars of the prison and touched hands with the shadow warriors at times, but there was always a degree of seperation. The shining souls that danced and laughed were so graceful and held such love that my heart wept that any of them had to suffer the gray battlefield, but now they were so happy it hurt to see them—I longed so much for the city of eternal love that they were in. For some reason, my eyes were drawn back to the cage. The shadows all had shining smiles and were laughing as they fought. I thought to myself, "I've never been much of a dancer."

When I woke up, the dream that had been so surreal was quickly fading. I tried to focus on it, but couldn't remember the motions of the graceful dancers or the shapes of the shadow warriors. An intolerable itch poked into my chest and I sat up, immediately regretting it. I tried to clear the horrible, thick sludge in my throat and Ferrin was there at my side. The others were watching me as I coughed and spat globs of blood onto the floor of the chamber. He handed me a canteen, from which I drank deeply. Cool water had never felt better going down my throat. The infernal itch was even forgotten for a few blessed seconds. I stopped drinking to get a breath, then closed my eyes and drank deeply again. Nothing hurt while I drank the clean, cold water.

When my thirst was sated, however, I had no choice but to face the brutal pain and itch that made me want to claw at my face to avoid scratching my chest. "What . . . in the . . . HELL . . . did you put on my chest?!" I croaked at Ferrin. The elf gently smiled, partly in relief and partly in condolence for my aggravation and agony. "You got the worst of it, but if it itches that badly it's a very good sign. That's your body healing it's wounds."

"You need to remember that now that your back you can't pass through solid objects like walls and Manticore claws and whatnot. If you die we'd have to carry all the useful stuff your holding.", Clay told me. Unfortunately, Clay's mouth had survived the ordeal. I would have told him how I felt about his comment if it wasn't a waste of breath. "I can walk if you help me up.", I said to the others. Drake and Ferrin obliged while I tried not to cry out. If felt like the claws were still there pressing against my lungs whenever I dared to breath. When I told Ferrin he said, "That's a good sign.", which I disagreed with. Apparently our healers had the right items with them to draw out poison and restore the individuals that had been affected. Michelle still seemed slightly out of it and she relied heavily on Elwin for support. Simon, though the healers had deemed him as fit as ever, looked worse for the experience. I didn't like the blank expression on his face as we kept going.

Nigel was in awe at Hebbeth's foresight and he was shaking his head in wonder as he went on about the brilliant design of the necromancer's dungeon and the idea of keeping his most powerful surprises hidden until he absolutely needed them. Clay told Nigel to shut his hole and we all voiced agreement (except for Simon, who I still had doubts had fully recovered his wits), although I'm fairly sure we were all impressed as to Hebbeth's planning. I was not looking forward to the next level of the dungeon, which was the floor on which we encountered the combination of the starving rats and the gore golems. William was far more shaken by Simon's condition than he was of the next challenge we could face at any moment. Thus far our skills in combat had overcome Hebbeth's stronger monsters, but the scope of his planning showed that there was no telling what surprise could be around any corner. We passed through the archway that had held the speed trap with care and waited for the axe to fall as we came to the stairs that we were now aware turned into a slope halfway down. Nigel explained the next floor to the new party members and I just spent the time dreading what was to come. "Once we reach the bottom of the slope here it's a lot harder to get back to this floor. Last time we cut some footholds but Hebbeth's dungeon repairs itself, so you don't have very long to get up the slope before it repairs itself and you slide back down.", he expounded on the details.

The going down was easy since near the bottom of the slope the hall was filled with murky water. I was quickly reminded of the menace we had faced before the gore golem or the rats; the bloodsucking insects. They were attracted to the strong scent of blood coming from me, too. We trekked through the corridors that still had stains on the walls and floor from the filth the gore golems were made of. Nigel searched his pack for something that would help us repel the swarming insects, but cursed when he couldn't find anything. "I just don't have anything with me that would help against them!" He growled, reclosing his pack and hefting it again. Vincent had his visor down and the others had tied pieces of cloth around their faces to block the insects from their mouths and noses. The insects were definitely much thicker on this level than before, and I dreaded to find out why. We made it about halfway to the next door when we turned a corner and found the next hallway to be blocked by some sort of clear slime. We couldn't see very far into it because the edge of it was filled with the insects and their eggs apparently.

Nigel's first priority after backing everyone else up was to hit the slime with his fire rings, which had been recharging for a while. The fire definitely sizzled and smoked, leaving a thin film of slime in the air and killing the bugs and their brood, but it didn't burn much of the slime. Before he used too much of his fire rings' energy, he stopped and examined the wall of slime closely. "I . . . I think we may have a problem.", Nigel told us. We could all see what the problem was already. The slime didn't just fill this part of the hall, it went all the way back to where the hall spit, and there was no way to tell how far we'd have to dig our way through this slime. Michelle just shook her head when Nigel asked if there was any spell that could remove all the slime at once.

All this time we had fought through the more deadly enemies and now we were going to be stopped by a damnable wall of slime. It was exasperating and infuriating, but we had to figure out a way to get through if we wanted to catch up to Hebbeth and his familiar. Nigel popped his neck and then produced the key from the exploding door. He had kept it all this time in the hopes it would prove useful as a trade item if nothing else. The fact that we had the key to the explosive door was another detail we might be able to use, but how would we get to the door? "I bet that explosive door would come in handy right now to get through here. Especially if we were on the other side of it.", he told us, his admiration of Hebbeth's planning disgusting our entire group all over again. "The explosive door already exploded, remember?", I reminded him.

"Yes,", he said, "But Hebbeth's dungeon is enchanted to reconstruct itself, so it should be back as long as he didn't use a spell to make the door explosive." I reflected on how dangerous magic was.

It was difficult to concentrate at all since, while we stood around thinking about how to get through, we were being slowly eaten alive by all the damned bugs. It was incredible how the details of Hebbeth's dungeon suddenly pushed their way to the top of the list of priorities when he chose for them to. As we stood there comtemplating, some of the bloodsuckers that escaped us went over to the slime and implanted their eggs again. Over the course of ten minutes, we all felt terrible, there were new batches of eggs in the slime, and then we heard the sound of slime sliding against a slick surface and the edge of the slime scooted out about five feet.

We were all preparing to run when it stopped. Michelle thought for a few seconds and then told us, "Five feet every ten minutes, if we are thirty minutes behind, should mean that this slime isn't very far, just this one tunnel at most." Nigel had already surrendered his pack and had a small spade out, digging through the slime pretty quickly. After close to eight minutes he had made it about seven feet that we could squeeze through and Michelle called for him to get out of it. In a couple more minutes, when the slime expanded again, is slurped and filled the space Nigel had dug out. Nigel swatted at the insects a couple of times, his face growing red, then he finally slammed the spade down in anger. "I'm out of ideas, people, so if you have a good idea you need to tell us!"

I thought back to when we were first on this floor and droplets had fallen from the ceiling a couple of times. Then it hit me. This slime had been on this level the entire time, it just hadn't had much nourishment. The bugs must have another source they were multiplying at if the slime moved up and ate the eggs planted in it every ten minutes. "Alright," I coughed, feeling the room begin to spin. I pressed a hand to the wall and interupted myself, "Woah. Dizzy." I kept a hand on the wall so I could keep my balance and finished what I had started to say, "Alright, the bugs are feeding the slime with their eggs. Where are the bugs actually coming from, then? Stop the source and starve the slime.", I guessed. Occasionally a piece of the slime would fall from the ceiling with a splat. When noone else came up with an alternate solution we backtracked to find the source of the insects, which we all assumed was the murky water we slid into when we first came off of the long spiral staircase to reach this level. The others had noticed my slow pace and how careful I was to keep a hand on the wall and eventually mentioned it. Ferrin asked, "Do your wounds still itch?" and I told him I itched all over. He frowned, saying, "This is no time for games. Most of the deaths I've seen were from infection. Do your chest wounds still itch as badly as they did at first?"

"They were worse than this before, yes.", I said. The healers looked at each other with grim faces and began pulling out vials and potions. "You are going to seriously do that right now? I said, making a face. I was leaning against the wall and slid down to sit on the floor, which was still covered in something red and slick. At this point resting was more important than avoiding something disgusting. They gave me a couple things to drink and then pulled me back to my feet to keep going. The dizziness eased up, but I felt weary. Axer slipped and cracked his backside on the hard floor. Growling in frustration, he got back to his feet in a few attempts and began swatting at the bugs. We ended up back at the entrance and Nigel used his ice rings to freeze the water. "That ought to stop the little pests." He said. I imagined Hebbeth had said the same thing when he helped the slime become larger. Nigel used the energy in his rings to burn all the bugs he could and then used all the rest of his ice power to refreeze the water. The bugs had been thinned out substantially, but how long would it take to starve the slime? Some of them lasted a long time between meals.

Michelle and William had been discussing spells and the different ways magic might be able to aid in clearing a way through the slime. William suggested that, based on the fact that it deadened flames, perhaps a bubble of force could be used to protect whoever was inside it and push the slime out of the way using a beam of some kind to push it. Michelle liked William's idea, but the problem was that in order to make a bubble big enough for someone to ride inside and still keep up the energy needed to prevent a beam from destroying it they would have to have more energy than they had. I snapped awake, realizing that I was dozing off despite how uncomfortable I was. They were still trying to think of a way to make it work when I felt weariness and pain overtake me.

I was awake again, but looking around something was different. I realized none of the bugs were bothering me. William happened to look over at me while the others were talking and shouted in alarm. Looking down, I saw the bugs covering my corpse. "Oh, That's just grand!", I said angrily. Michelle's eyes lit up and it looked like she was crazy as she looked at the tunnel, looked down calculating, then looked at me and back at the tunnel and finally at the others. The healers were already shooing the bloodsuckers off my corpse to try to restore my life, but Michelle said, "Wait! This is just what we need!"

The Healers looked over at her and then at each other, confused. Michelle told us, "Jordas can pass through the slime now!"

I just groaned.

A smaller bubble to hold the key was made and Simon seemed to be slowly coming around as they got ready to push the key through the slime. They blasted the bubble holding the key and pushed it to where there was a bend in the hall. Once that was done, it would be up to me from there. In order to have the energy I needed to semi-possess the key and pull it through that goo I had to feed. The others formed a barrier to try to keep the bugs away. They were going to wait while I got through the tunnel and reached the door. I sunk through the floor to the next level down in order to look for prey. There were a couple of giant spiders I found, but other than that everything else seemed to have escaped. As a rule, insects don't have very much energy to drain. Still low on energy and unable to run across anything else after searching for twenty minutes, I decided to see just how far I could pull the key and what it would accomplish. I went to where the key was on the floor the party was waiting at and possessed it with my hand, then put everything I had into dragging it through the goo.

I didn't usually pay much attention to the energy I spent passing through walls and floors, but moving myself through the slime made me realize just how much energy it took to do so. At the time it was more than I could spare, but the only other option was to find some insects and that would take too long to refill my energy. I was a couple more corridors away from where I thought I remembered the explosive door being and got a very bad feeling. I hadn't been attacked by a demon in so long that I had, thankfully, forgotten the details of the experience. This very bad feeling was my warning sign that an evil spirit was near. I felt weak for having low energy, but I thought back to what Ferrin said about demons not bothering you if you aren't worth the trouble. I thought of purity and happiness and good and filled myself with purpose right before I saw an apparition become visible. It looked like a knight in heavy, darkened armor. His helmet had two black horns sticking out of it and his hands appeared to be claws. I let go of the key and used all the energy I could muster to push myself through the wall into the the corridor behind the demon and when I came out on the other side of the wall he was right behind me. In spirit form, you don't really feel pain. Usually.

This demon's touch brought pain to my spirit, and I yelped and continued pushing through the goo to get back to my allies. I couldn't push myself through any more walls. The demon was right behind me and closing the distance. I thought of what Ferrin had told me again as I fled from it. There was no way I could outrun the demon, so I finally concentrated on my courage and stopped to face it. Hey, I thought to myself, if it's a spirit it must have energy, too! I could take it's energy!

When I turned to face it, it wasn't there. I felt those claws jab into my back and lunged away from them, turning to face my enemy. "I won't be worth the trouble.", I told the evil spirit in a determined voice. He approached me again and said, "It's no trouble at all." With all my strength I reached out to draw energy from him. It only took a moment for him to realize what was happening, and when he did realize it, he sped up considerably. I drew back and put all my power into one two-handed swing and caught the foe with the hit perfectly, sending him reeling. The demon's eye slits flared red and I had a moment of clarity as he charged at me. When I attacked not with anger or hatred but to defend myself, they never seemed to be able to stop me. Ferrin had been right, it was my energy and anger that had fed them. Long ago this tortured spirit may have been my friend. For the first time I felt more pity rather than fear and compassion instead of hate. With these feelings in my heart I tried to consider a way that I could help the man trapped within that unholy shell. He rushed at me but his charge broke when I began to glow. The closer he struggled toward me, the less progress he made.

'It works!', I thought to myself. The wonder of it brought a smile to my face and I told the demon warrior, "There is such a thing as mercy. Just act on what you feel is right."

He stopped and the red glow disappeared from his eyes and he blinked at me as if I'd just lost my mind. He tried to slash at me again, but was held out of reach by the light emanating from me. He lowered his hands since claws wouldn't work and simply stared at me trying to figure out what to do. "We could be friends instead of enemies.", I told him. Shaking his head as if giving up on understanding, a portal opened with flames bursting out of it and he dropped into the opening, which immediately closed up leaving nothing to show he had been there. The glow of light slowly faded, but I no longer felt weak. When Ferrin had spoken to me about it my response had been the same; I hadn't understood and thought him a fool. I had lived three lifetimes while he had only lived part of one, how could he have more wisdom than me?

Now I saw the arrogance in that attitude and wondered at how arrogant we all are, thinking we know so much.

I dragged the key the rest of the way to the door and then pressed it into the indentation where it was supposed to go. With a nasty sound, slime spilled through the doorway into the room made of glowing blue stones with a well in the middle. 'Well, here I am.', I thought. Hebbeth walked in from an adjacent chamber and spotted me. His eyes opened wide and he scrambled back through the doorway. I smiled, feeling invincible, and approached. From the next room I heard Hebbeth's angry voice shouting at me, "I found an old friend of yours!", and almost silently a large white and gray form padded into the chamber. The giant wraith! I backed toward the slime-filled passage and laughed. How perfect this was! The ghoul would give chase, pushing through the slime-filled passage and clearing the corridors the entire way back!

The intention was certainly to give chase as it bounded across the room at me, leaping over the well in the middle. At first I thought it was going to catch me because it moved so easily through the slime. It wasn't long before the strength required to push through all that slime began to wane. I felt good—I felt great! I started passing through walls and when I reached my compatriots I informed them that the giant wraith was on it's way and that it was clearing the way for us. The team had to back around the next corner to make certain noone was hit by all the traps we laid for the wraith. Explosive vials, magic glyphs and spells, and everything else anyone could think of that would hurt the big monster. The sound of the wraith breaking through the end of the slime and the resounding explosions were sweet, indeed. Then it began triggering glyphs that would slow and harm it with fire, electricity, and acid. The clerics and Ferrin worked together to form a big sphere of light so bright it hurt my eyes to look at it. When the fiend rounded the corner, it got slammed by the biggest blast of holy energy this side of eternity. The energy from it filled me with a warm reassurance. All was right with the world. The wraith was gone except for a scorched spot.

We cheered and congratulated each other and danced around and filled that little part of the dungeon with a celebration that none of us would forget. Those in the party that had never fought the wraith were still surprised how much punishment it had taken to destroy it. They couldn't know how great a challenge they had just overcome, though. Certanius spun in the air and Axer danced around shouting gleefully. Ferrin and Nigel laughed and did a complicated set of salutes and handshakes which I assumed were saved for only the most important victories. I danced around like an idiot drunk on life's joys, too. Our victory dance didn't last long, but it was a good one!

"Hebbeth is already back!", I suddenly remembered aloud. We ran through the slime-covered halls (looking back that wasn't a good idea, but noone fell) and when we got to the blue room Hebbeth had barricaded his door. We stood back while the Possessed slammed on the door until they jarred something on the other side. There was a deafening explosion and when the dust cleared we saw that the possessed were in a scorched heap on the opposite side of the chamber.

Hebbeth came dashing through the doorway and screamed a wordless battle cry. He was a vicious, bloodthirsty, and selfish man, but none would ever call him a fool or a coward. We all knew when he came charging out that this was his last effort to remove our party, which stood as his only obstacle, and he would not go quietly. I had no time left to admire him, the fight was on and would end in this blue-glowing room.

Chapter 7

Laughter is the cure

Hebbeth had dressed in clothing that was better suited to combat. Close-fitting light plate armor with chain mail beneath it. He had a sword in each hand and over the armor he wore several devices bearing glyphs and runes that glowed or made dangerous sounds. Axer threw Certanius, who began spinning almost as fast as before and changed direction as it neared the necromancer. Hebbeth pointed a device on his wrist at Certanius and a burst of hurricane wind caught the axe and bounced it off the back wall. Certanius let us all know, <I'm out of energy! Flank him!>

Hebbeth was moving faster than he had before, so he must have enchanted himself with a haste spell. Clay and Vincent advanced side by side and Hebbeth threw himself right at them, his swords spinning and slashing through the air so quickly that he steadily pushed them both back. Drake whipped around with his scythe and Hebbeth rolled to the side and then fired a short beam at the ceiling above Drake. We all heard the sound of shattering magic as Hebbeth disenchanted the regenerative properties of the bricks he had struck, and immediately following his first move he pointed with one finger and a device on his shoulder twisted slightly and launched a small fireball to the spot Hebbeth pointed at, which was the disenchanted area of bricks. Drake backpedaled to avoid being squashed under the falling rocks, but Nigel launched himself forward into the air and seemed to grab at something as the loosened stones crashed down on and around him. Ferrin managed to snap out a kick and connected with Hebbeth's back. In fast motion, the necromage regained his balance and spun around with both swords out. Ferrin backflipped to avoid having his head chopped off. Michelle sent a bombardment of ice knives from the pool in the middle of the room and Hebbeth guarded for just a split second and then began dashing around the pool toward her. She moved the stream of tiny, piercing projectiles in front of Hebbeth and he had to begin zigzagging to avoid the attack. Clay and Vincent simply couldn't keep up with his movements. He had only been nicked by a few of the shards, but due to the haste spell more blood escaped before his body was able to heal.

William loosed a few arrows, missing, and then dropped the bow and began to cast a haste spell of his own, drawing his sword. Elwin must have used up all his energy to heal the Possessed, because he fell to one knee and then sat against the wall as the Felltower and Martin stood. "Hebbeth, you will die, traitor!", Felltower threatened. The possessed moved with fantastic speed toward Hebbeth, and the necromage slashed downward in a brutal attack that opened Michelle from shoulder to side. She simply gasped as she fell down. Hebbeth leaped into the air and the Possessed also jumped, but Hebbeth pointed and nearly all of the magical devices he had fired spells off. The possessed were hit by two lightning bolts, a fireball, and something dark that attached itself to the possessed—some sort of curse! The possessed were already incapacitated again and seemed not to be healing as quickly as they usually did. Vincent swung a full-fledged killing blow right at Hebbeth's back that only struck the floor as Hebbeth spun around and stunned him with a lightning blast from one of his spellcasting gadgets.

I simply was unable to move fast enough to catch Hebbeth as he sped around fighting. Drake went to heal Michelle and Hebbeth started for him and suddenly everything slowed down. I looked over to William, who had his arms outstretched to me and opened his eyes as he finished saying something. Sounds were slower, deeper. It looked like Hebbeth was the only one moving close to a regular speed. I propelled myself at the necromage as he ran Drake through with both blades and he looked up toward William and raised his hand to point at the boy. I saw one of the lightning bolt launchers begin to glow and the runes and glyphs flashed in it as a blue charge formed around the end of it. I threw myself into Hebbeth, trying to possess his body, and small tendrils of electric exploded in all directions as Hebbeth fought for control of his own body. He and I both screamed as our souls grappled to gain the advantage, and the sound of both screams came from the body we were fighting in.

Hebbeth and I circled each other, trying to force one another outside the bounds of the body. <I am going to tear your soul apart and send each

piece to a corner of the ocean!> Hebbeth cried within the confines of his mind. <You won't do anything like that ever again because I'm stopping you NOW!>, I told him as I pushed with all my strength. I felt his alarm, but the nearness of his defeat increased the intensity of his struggling, and he shoved me backward and retook control of his body.

No sooner did we find ourselves seperated again than the sorcerer jumped away from me and fired that barely visible curse at me. I would have avoided it if I could, but it had the width of a net and clung to me like syrup. It definitely was less sweet than syrup. The curse boggled my mind and made me feel weak and confused. It made me feel like the control of my movements were backwards. I wanted to get close to Hebbeth and steal his energy, but began flying backward.

Hebbeth ran to where William was healing Drake and raised his swords to kill the young man, but the Possessed slammed into Hebbeth's back running at full speed. With two minds and a few extra seconds, they had figured out the basic movements even if they couldn't grab onto the necromancer. The bullrush had knocked him onto his face, and he scrambled to his feet and rushed toward William again just as the boy was finishing healing Drake, who was coughing up blood even though he was getting back to his feet. The Possessed ran straight at Hebbeth just to slow him down and he brought the swords back on opposite sides. Martin must have noticed at the same time I did, because one leg locked up on the Possessed and Hebbeth missed with his decapitating scissor-strike. The Possessed rolled and slid on the ground, and Hebbeth couldn't leap fast enough to avoid tripping. As William and Drake backed away picking up their sword and scythe to face Hebbeth, Simon let an arrow fly and hit the necromancer in the side as he rose. Clay kept trying to get a bead on Hebbeth for a cut, but since everyone was so close that he couldn't get a solid oppurtunity he taunted Hebbeth by saying, "You got the point, I see."

Hebbeth gritted his teeth and winced in pain, then turned with an evil look on his face and enunciated a word I couldn't understand. It must have been a curse he perfected to take only one word to cast. Something red flew through the air toward Simon, repeatedly dissappearing and reappearing. Simon had notched another arrow when the spell struck him in the hands. Immediately, blisters appeared all over his hands and Simon began to shake as his eyes rolled back into his head and he fell over, his skin turning an angry red and blisters continuing to appear.

I had sort of gotten the hang of moving around and started to float toward Hebbeth again, but then the curse wore off and suddenly I was moving backwards again. I had to forget what I had just learned in order to move normally again! Meanwhile, Hebbeth drove William and Drake toward the wall and the Possessed got back up. Axer came running up behind Hebbeth with Certanius in one hand and Hebbeth knocked both the boy and the cleric off balance and spun to cut horizontally in the air. The mage had forgotten there was a goblin fighting here, too, and he had aimed his slashes too high. Axer called out, "LEGBREAKER!", and jabbed his little goblin hand into the same knee he had hit before. As Hebbeth toppled over he screamed, "OAHHH!"

Axer jumped onto Hebbeth's armor plated chest and swung Certanius at Hebbeth's face. Using both swords, Hebbeth blocked the axe. Strangely, he seemed to be struggling against Axer's might. When Axer let go of the axe and began trying to pry Hebbeth's fingers loose from one of his swords, I realized that Certanius must have had more energy than he thought. Instead of anything fancy, he simply pushed against the necromancer's swords, effectively pinning him to the floor. Drake wasted no time in aiming at middle of Hebbeth's forehead with a stab from the tip of his scythe. Clay lashed out with his longsword as well.

Hebbeth had to be growing stronger, I realized. He had taken so much punishment and continued to struggle. Recalling how much power he had gained when he had absorbed the hatred of my friend, Harvey, I searched my own heart. I didn't hate Hebbeth any more, I just wanted to stop the terrible things he had been doing. As shocked as I was to find this out about myself, I examined the others for signs of evil intent and had to say by the look on Drake's face that it was obvious his emotions were one source of Hebbeth's extra power. I didn't even have time to call out—Drake's scythe sped downward and Hebbeth twisted his body, barely deflecting the scythe and simultaneously moving Certanius so that the axe wouldn't be able to keep him on his back. The rolling motion might not have detached Axer, but the necromage released his grasp on his sword and Axer let go of Hebbeth to steal the sword.

Axer raised the sword in both hands (for a human it was a long sword, but for a goblin it was a gigantic greatsword) and took his 'stance', then looked right into Hebbeth's eyes and commanded, "BE AFRAID, DUMB HEBBETH THE LEGBROKEN! YOU NOW FACE AXER, WHO STOLE THE MAGIC AXE AND SLAYED THE GIANT WIZARD! THE

SAME AXER WHO HAS TWICE BROKEN THE NECROMANCER'S LEG AND CUT OFF THE OLD MAN'S SPINY TAIL! YES, BUTT UGLY HEBBETH, THE SAME AXER WHO SURVIVERED YOUR THOUSANDS DEATH RATS AND YOUR BIG UGLY MONSTER WITH THE BUTT BREATH OF DEATH!"

The entire fight stopped for one second and Hebbeth actually started laughing. Ferrin stepped out from Hebbeth's right side without a sound and jabbed him in the throat, a perfect martial arts strike cutting off the sound of Hebbeth's laughter. Hebbeth fell to his knees, but Axer was right there with the sword and Hebbeth fell on his own sword. Before blood was even pouring from his mouth he was choking on laughter. The irony of his own death. The sound he made before dying was a whine halfway between crying and laughing. Clay made certain by running his blade through Hebbeth's back. He wasn't the only one; Drake, William and I all tried our best to elicit a response from the corpse by attacking it.

Nigel's muffled cries of pain came from the huge pile of rocks near the edge of the chamber and while Vincent and Clay shifted the stones off of him, The others were able to help Michelle regain conciousness even though she had been severely wounded. The healing magic was all used up at the moment, so regular steps were taken to keep her alive. Simon was dead as a doornail, and our two warriors moved the fallen stones over the old man's body to provide a respectful resting place. There were plenty of worse places than the glowing blue room for a funeral, so that's what we did once the others were as safe as possible. The spell Hebbeth had hit the old man with had boiled his blood, which Michelle told us was not lethal normally in that small of a time, but the strain on Simon's heart had apparently been too much.

Nigel winced with every breath as he explained his earlier actions. "I had a lens that was made to detect magical things. I had—ungh—forgotten that I had it with me. I put it on when I found it and was able to see Hebbeth's familiar and-", he stopped to grimace, "Ow. Anyway, I tried to capture it so that we wouldn't have to worry about it calling Hebbeth's soul back. Which—Ow, DAMNIT that hurt! Ungh! Which I did catch it, but I think the bricks that fell . . . well . . . we won't be interrogating it, we'll put it that way! Ha, ha—OUCH! Why couldn't these bricks fall on you instead?", he asked Clay. The smartalec responded with a question of his own, which was, "Waaa, why wouldn't wees wicks wall won woo?", in a mocking tone.

We had finally managed to corner Hebbeth and his familiar and destroy them. We had lost Slop and Simon in our efforts. Nigel left the less valuable items he had behind and packed up the rare tomes and spells he could find in Hebbeth's chamber. Clay and Vincent hadn't been carrying much of anything but loaded their packs with everything else they could find. We refilled our water canteens and started back out of the dungeon the way we came.

Other than the bothersome insects on the rat level, nothing else decided to test our combat skills. One of the items that had been loaded up in a special container was Hebbeth's head for proof of our efforts even though Certanius assured us that it would not be necessary. Axer wielded Certanius in one hand and Hebbeth's sword in the other and tried to pick a fight whenever we saw another lifeform (or undead form) at a distance, but could not goad anything into attacking us. Eventually he began reciting his title in practice for the next great battle where he would announce his presence. William and the others spoke fondly of the sayings our fallen ally had told them and the knowledge he had helped them to develop. At one point there was a silence and William asked, "Which one of you will I stay with now?" Uneasily Michelle and Vincent looked at each other. Elwin put a hand on the boy's shoulder and smiled sadly. "You can stay with me if you'd like, Will. Are you still sure the life of an adventurer is what you want for yourself?"

Surprisingly, William didn't respond for quite a while. He seemed to be thinking about it for a few levels as we grew ever closer to the surface again. When noone else said anything, Vincent began to sing a song he had picked up someplace.

Long ago I travelled as a merchant on the sea.
I never bowed to anyone—I was absolutely free!
As years went on I found that there still had been cost.
The work I did would all be gone the day that I was lost.

So I sold my sailor's hat and bought myself a sword.
I'd save good folks and lay fiends low to please my rightful lord!
One day I came to realize that laws were made by men.

And swords were true, that much was sure, but laws could be broken.

Ashamed I'd been so quickly duped, I threw my sword away!
Although men's laws could be broken, God's law was here to stay!
I begged forgiveness night and day, for sins long in my past.
I learned that words are nothing, that our *actions* have to last.

With no real skill but my body and will,
I'll search 'til life makes sense.
At times with an oar or a prayer or a sword,
I'll make a difference!

"Where did you learn that?", Will asked him. Vincent smiled and said, "Over the last thirty years or so I picked up pieces here and there." Will was awestruck. "I didn't know you used to sail! Wow, where did you serve a lord?", Will wondered aloud more than directing the question to Vincent, but the heavily laden warrior responded anyway. Adjusting the pack he carried, Vincent told Will, "I thought you might have listened more carefully, Will. I don't really want to talk about those I served—they weren't nice people."

Will didn't ask anything else, but it was easy to see that the boy looked on Vincent with admiration.

The uncomfortable quiet was broken soon by Clay, who jested, "My favorite verse was the one about having no real skill."

Vincent scowled at him and Clay just grinned at him. Clay chuckled to himself as Vince just adjusted the overloaded pack he carried.

We were back to ground level and approaching the doorway leading out when it occurred to me that I still hadn't left this plane of existence even though Hebbeth was no more. Ferrin noticed that I was wearing a funny look and had apparently been thinking about the same thing. He walked next to me and questioned me about it. "What are you waiting for?", He asked solemnly. Vincent grunted ahead of us, "What? Sorry, I couldn't understand you. What did you ask?"

Ferrin patted him on his free shoulder, "Nevermind, Vincent, I was speaking with our ghostly friend here."

Vince asked, "I thought you were leaving after Hebbeth was taken care of. Was there someone else you had to find first?"

Ferrin nodded and I couldn't decide why I was still here. "I can't decide what is keeping me here.", I told him. "I just feel like I'm not ready to go yet.", I tried to think of anything else that might hold me here, but nothing came to mind. Ferrin just smiled knowingly and said, "All in good time."

Elwin began humming the tune Vince had been singing earlier and we all walked out of the dungeon into the starlight. The path we walked was quiet, the night calm around us as we ventured for the nearest civilization. According to Michelle's estimation it would take us about a day and a half to reach the closest town. Felltower voiced his concern that the humans would kill him, but Michelle promised him that she would find a way to restore his life and seperate Martin from him. She also let Martin and I know that she would be seeking out a priest in one of the great temples so that our bodies could be manifested for us again.

As the morning dawned we could see a huge pillar of black smoke in the sky in the direction we were headed. Clay cursed intermittently throughout the day and his foul mood darkened all our spirits. We continued and increased our pace a bit to reach the smoldering town before noon. The town was little more than a smoking scorch mark on the landscape. The rotting dead lay in gruesome positions throughout the town. Almost all of them had been burned at least partially. I did not envy Michelle's ability as a seer since so many had been slaughtered here. I wondered how many ghosts had been left as a result of the massacre. It wasn't a total loss, though, as we also found two dead lizardmen.

We hurried through the remains of the town toward the nearest city and I noticed a change in the way the undead lizardman in our group was moving. "Martin?" I asked to see if he had taken control of the body. "Yes, it's me.", he said. "Felltower is becoming . . . more alert. He's preparing himself for battle and if I am not mistaken I believe he intends to kill us.", Martin told us.

Ferrin's eyebrows were raised and Nigel cleared his throat and said, "Ah huh. So, uh . . . Felltower, Why do you want to kill us?"

Instead of Felltower responding, Martin explained hesitantly as if he was relaying the information from someone else and he had to pause in between to listen to what they said. "According to writings that have been passed down for thousands of years, there used to be a lot more dragons in the world. In their fear of the dragons' superior size and power, Humans began to hunt down and kill off the stronger race. The dragons of that time made a pact to avenge their kind against the humans and they began to war against men."

Pausing as we passed a tree where many birds were singing, he nodded in understanding and then continued, "As with all wars, vile acts were committed on both sides. Some of the younger dragons made a habit of capturing women for their own pleasure, and since dragons are highly magical, their . . . habits resulted in offspring that they decided to nuture. The war between the dragons and men went in favor of the humans, and dragons became rare. However, despite the bad blood between humans and the dragon spawns known as lizardmen, the great war eventually faded from memory since so few dragons remained to hunt down. Lizardmen are still shunned by humans, and many are still fighting the great war, but must hide in order to avoid being hunted down and overwhelmed by the humans, who have superior numbers." Martin stopped and opened his canteen for a long drink of water while Axer climbed an apple tree and tossed the others some apples. When he came down he had five apples for himself. As we kept going, our moods improved a bit.

Martin shook his head and a short time later told us, "Felltower is a member of a clan of lizardmen that took to hiding deep in Hebbeth's dungeon along with three other clans of lizardmen. They are led by an ancient dragon named Sissoks and were planning to attack humans when they were strong enough. Felltower is certain that attack has begun and wants me to let you all know that you don't have to worry at all. When we cross paths with the next group of lizardmen we need only turn ourselves in peacefully and we will be allowed to live—and we won't be tortured, either."

Michelle angrily said, "Alright, Will, Elwin, Drake, we're going to rid ourselves of one lizard right now.", and the possessed froze in place. Martin came across, "I'm trying to hold him—it's not easy! Get on with it!"

The body was trembling as Michelle and William cast a spirit-seperation and the two clerics stood behind each of them channelling their energy into the two spellcasters. Simon had used his intellect to avoid using as much energy, but Michelle used her energy like a hammer, simply overpowering the spirit she wanted to pull out. The spell took much less time Michelle's way, but as Ferrin told me while they were casting it would drain the energy from all four of them to complete the spell that way. When it was done Felltower was gone.

"At least I didn't have to cut his heart out again.", Vincent said in relief. He wasn't the only one who was relieved. Heart removal was a long process that was almost as painful to be present for as it was for the victim. We continued onward with a lot of hope that the dragon went in a different direction than we were travelling. Axer asked us, "We need to grab birds and train them, don't we?"

"Why in the world would you think of training birds right now?", Ferrin wondered. Axer put emphasis on every word as if Ferrin was a complete lackwit, "To KILL the DRAGON!", and then Axer shook his head as if to say 'why are you so stupid?' to Ferrin. The elf was shaking his head, too, awestruck at such a ridiculous plan. "How would a bird even harm a dragon?", Ferrin asked Axer.

Axer sighed as if explaining every detail were tedious to him (other than Ferrin, everyone else was enjoying the topic as it took their minds off of walking) and went on to explain that the birds would pick us up so that we could fly after the dragon to avoid it escaping. Clay smacked his forehead and began digging in his pack. Michelle rolled her eyes, already awaiting the punchline when Axer turned to Clay and asked what he had thought of. "We have no need to train birds, we can purchase birds that are already trained!" and Axer shouted victoriously before pointing a finger in Ferrin's face and letting him have it with, "HAHA! Stupid elf! See, someone smart already thought of that!"

Clay counted out four coins then said, "Well, we can use the reward from Hebbeth I suppose. We also need to disguise ourselves and I suppose it would take about fifty birds per person. Of course, we won't be able to wear any armor and we'll have to buy lighter weapons."

Axer listened carefully to Clay's list of items needed for a bird-to-dragon assault and blinked, realizing something that didn't make sense. "Why do we need disguises?", Axer asked. Clay explained that the birds he was thinking of were trained as message carriers, so we'd have to be rolled up in big tubes of paper. Axer was still trying to work out the details when Michelle patted Axer's shoulder and told him, "Don't worry about it, Axer, we'll find another way to get the dragon", and then glared at Clay.

As we approached the city we were glad to see that it still stood and seemed unaffected by Sissoks' war. We quickly found out that there was no way in hell the guards were going to allow in a shade, a goblin, or a lizardman into the city. So we stayed outside while the others went into town. "Well, at least I have scales over my body now.", Martin said, looking on the bright side. I simply stood there mindlessly for the night as normal, but I made certain that I was facing the city gate so that the guards would be unnerved. As the morning sun began to rise, I felt the extra energy from the sun. When I had first left the dungeon I had thought I wouldn't need to feed in the daylight, but I was mistaken. I felt a bit weaker than I had yesterday and the sunlight, although it slowed the process of my energy being used up, did not stop it.

The group came out shortly before noon and they didn't have Elwin or Clay with them. Vincent was carrying a large sack of coins, though. Tied to his belt, the bag holding Hebbeth's head still appeared to be full. Will told us the good news, "When we showed them Hebbeth was dead, they gave us the reward and told us that we should try the other cities in this area as several had rewards on Hebbeth!

Michelle showed us the other side of the coin, though. "Elwin decided he was going to stay in the city because he's tired of travelling. He told us he's going to retire.", and she giggled. In a moment she grew serious again though. "Clay, that scoundrel, told us he had no intention of hunting down a dragon and advised us not to, either. Good riddance.", she sounded annoyed, but that made the 'good riddance' less convincing. At any rate, we had lost another two people and Vincent let us know that he was going to head toward the port further north and visit his hometown but would accompany us to the next city northeast if we wanted to go there next. We all were happy to have Vincent with us and would regret his absence when he was gone.

The journey to the next city wasn't a long one, but when it takes days to reach a place it always seems like a long time. Vincent had never spoken much, but Michelle coerced a bit of his history. The song he had sung to us before was a fair summary of his life. He had been more of a rapscallion when he sailed the sea and after several wars had realized his liege lord was causing more problems than he was solving, so he took up a sword and tried to work his way into becoming a paladin. The paladins had the notion that one had to be brought in from an early age, however. They offered to pay him to assist in guarding the young ones on their way to the paladin headquarters—a sad note that some unscrupulous characters would slaughter kids who *might* become paladins so that there were less of them to interfere in the dark deeds that proved profitable. Vincent had turned them down, though. "If I'm to help, teach me your skills so that I may help as much as possible.", he had urged the paladin he spoke with. She had said no, though. The paladins had a strong reputation, and they had to protect it by preventing anyone from becoming a paladin who might be hiding bad intentions. They had even refused to let him prove himself in the trials of their order.

He hadn't always looked up to the paladins, but now had the utmost respect for their order. He decided he didn't need their training. The abilities they had to heal others or drive off evil spirits would not be available to him, but he suspected that his skill in combat was as great as theirs. After that point he had been hunting for jobs so that he could feed himself and when he had learned of Hebbeth he had decided the necromage had to be stopped. He was the last to join the group when they were looking for help in the matter, but had proven himself several times over. Martin, Axer and I encountered the same situation as before in the next city. Vincent parted ways with us the next morning, heading north. His armor had never shined like a paladin's armor, but as the sun gleamed off of it as we lost sight of him, we knew that he was a paladin in every way except title.

The plan was to reach the largest city in this area and find a way to get us (the nonhumans) inside so that we could take some time to rest up and find a way to bring Sissoks down. We didn't voice our agreement, but it was implied since noone spoke up against hunting down the dragon and stopping his war of revenge. Michelle passed the time reading while Drake and Martin spoke and Will asked me questions about heaven (I don't remember), hell (I don't want to remember), and being a ghost. I explained as best I could how it felt to pass through solid matter and as he grew more comfortable with the subject he began asking tougher questions about what sort of things had enough energy to sustain me, how long it took to run out of energy, and the philosophical ramifications of draining out another being's energy to sustain oneself. When the conversation reached that point, I realized I was speaking to a child about these complex ideas and was struck speechless for a minute.

"Who have you studied under that you know so much about the world at such a young age, Will?", I asked. This boy had been travelling for his entire life. He had studied not only under Simon and Michelle, but had been trained in advanced healing arts and spells, had knowledge of battle tactics in addition to philosophy and anatomy, and had studied under at least two martial arts masters. William was welcomed wherever he went, he received food and shelter free of charge most of the places he ventured to and was a celebrity of great renown. Will was a one of a kind prodigy in every field he had studied. He could read and understood mathematics in world where most couldn't. There was a tinge of sadness to Will that noone seemed to be able to reach, though. The feeling when one looked at him was that he understood everything the world allowed him to perceive, and despite being loved by many, he was utterly alone.

We travelled for nearly a week to reach the great city, De'Lujean. In that time I learned that Drake was a staunch cleric of the order of the white scythe, which charged it's members with hunting down evil and sickness and vanquishing both. Drake was thirty five years old and had been in the order for ten years. There wasn't much else to be said about him as he had been spending all of his time chasing after monsters and healing the sick.

Michelle was a long time student of the arcane arts and hadn't always excelled in the teachings of magic. Over time she had gained much better control of her abilities than others her own age and specialized in using magic to open up a wider perception so that she could sometimes glimpse future events and could identify magical properties of an item or place if they had any. I thought that was pretty impressive to learn—I had gotten my vision the easy way; by dying.

I reminisced with Martin about some of the close calls we'd had in Hebbeth's dungeon before even Slop had been around. He told me he'd been there so long he couldn't remember who he'd been or what he'd done before. "Honestly I've no idea what I'll do once we have taken care of Sissoks. I've considered several professions, but none appeal to me.", Martin said. "You should definitely take advantage of one of your fast movements.", I laughed, "Can you imagine planting a field in a day when it would take someone else and three of their friends a week?"

Martin laughed with me, but shook his head, "There's no way I could do that. Whenever I do one of the fast motions you are talking about it really wears me out—and with muscles you get terrible cramps a little while afterward. Yes, at least until I'm a skeleton again I guess I won't bother with those. I'll just be your average farmer lizardman."

For some reason the image seemed ludicrous and we both chuckled.

When other subjects had run dry I asked Axer about how he'd come across Certanius' axe. Axer covered his eyes and slowly brought his hands away as he began his story, “Was darkest place ever! Then, Axer started to wake up and saw dark place. There were crawly bugs and stinky slimes all over, but Axer got by them and found a room with a door. There was goblins sleepin’ all over. Axer sneaked over and found a big rock.”

At that point he mimicked himself picking up a large rock and hefting it above his head. “Axer stood next to sleepin’ goblin who had axe and bumped him awake.”, he kicked the dust gently at his feet and then grinned in a big happy face and slammed the imaginary rock down. “Axer *SMACKED* out the goblin holdin’ axe and then grabbed the axe and RAN when the other gobbies were wakin’ up.”, his story was over but it had seemed unfinished, so he said, “The end.”

That was certainly an epic tale, I thought to myself. <Indeed.>, Certanius also thought to myself.

Chapter 8

Breakthrough

De'Lujean was no longer the glorious center of trade it had once been (at least according to Michelle) when we reached it. By reaching it I don't really mean reaching it so much as reaching the outskirts of the lizardman army besieging it. De'Lujean was a fortress of incredible proportions, with reinforced domes filling up the sky.

"Just like in the time of the plague!", William said excitedly. Nigel nodded in awe and agreement, "Yep, they activated the city's defenses again. Forget vampires—there's no way even a dragon can break that shield, either. It's had enchantments woven into it every day by the builders' guild to strengthen the old spells, and they scour the walls to repair areas that need to be sealed all the time, as well. It's part of their duty in addition to making certain that the roads in De'Lujean are in top shape."

Ferrin smiled as he said, "It reminds me of my homeland. So proud our victories stand, giving hope to the dreams of the young and shaping their future by sharing the awe of the triumphs of dedication."

"I'm glad it's still standing, as well. A siege doesn't really give us anywhere to go, though.", I said. You couldn't help but admire the amazing amount of work that the place would demand in upkeep, much less how much work had gone into it over the course of centuries. Unfortunately no matter how much work had been done on it, that didn't change our location, and I figured that the fact that we needed a place to rest should hold our attention right now as it was the more important topic.

The besiegers stayed well away from the walls of the city, and we saw why. There were a few blackened skeletons of lizardmen who had been too close when the defenses had been turned on. Michelle explained that the defenses were powered by mages from within the city and would use prepared spells to blast any invaders who were close enough. The lizardmen had taken many people as slaves and were using them as bait to draw out fighters from the city by torturing them out in the open. It was crude, evil, and infuriating: Just the kind of thing that would provoke the defenders to leave the safety of their walls. Some of the victims screamed and some begged for mercy (from their torturers or those in the city).

"I have an idea.", I told the others. "Remember the backward summoning portal idea?", I asked. Nigel started looking through his pack to find the papers about summoning. I asked Michelle if she knew whether the walls of the city would keep me out since I was able to pass through solid material. She had no idea, though. "Spirits have never been an enemy that De'Lujean has ever had to fight.", she said, "The domes aren't as old as the rest of the city, though. They were added after news of the dragon attacks reached them, so the defenses are usually prepared as soon as a great danger is realized."

"So I can probably get inside. The next part could be our undoing if we don't find someone trustworthy—Who do you know within the city that you are willing to trust with our souls? If we pull off this reverse-summon to get inside De'Lujean we still need someone inside to 'summon' us. We can only get halfway inside by ourselves."

I really hoped they truly knew someone we could entrust ourselves with. Nigel and Michelle discussed it for a little while and decided that each of them had one good idea for someone to contact who would be able to do the summoning portal.

In the deep night I slowly made my way through the sleeping army. Whenever a guard looked my direction I sank into the ground to hide. After giving them a minute I would peek out and see if the guard was still looking in my direction. When they weren't, I moved as quietly and quickly as I could. It didn't take a skilled soldier to recognize well-kept weaponry. To forge weapons and armor for all these lizardmen would have taken generations. The more I thought about it, the more frightening the thought was. If the Dragon had planned this out, generations of lizardmen could have been used to create all the weaponry and items, and then almost all of the new generation could have been trained to use it. If the training was repeated over another generation or two, it would be a religion of combat.

I snapped out of it. While I'm dreaming our foe's mightier and mightier I might as well picture them all as dragons. I smiled to myself. Now THAT'S a scary thought!

I reached the wall of De'Lujean and pushed myself through. The walls were so thick it took me five seconds to pass all the way through. Even at night in the middle of a siege the city was busy, with people shouting and dancing and selling wares. I wondered how anyone could sleep in such a place and searched for the temple where one of the people Michelle and Nigel had indicated was supposed to make her home here. Many were absorbed in their own affairs, but those who saw me were making a fuss, so I tried to avoid the main roads. I rounded a corner in a back alley and two young people who were . . . ahem . . . enjoying themselves . . . stopped and stared in shock. I couldn't help but give them an ominous smile and then continue on.

Guards were being called to find out where this ghost was—guards with magical abilities. I began to cross the main road right in front of the temple and I heard a deep voice from above shout, "He's in front of the temple!"

I hurried toward the temple but was curious why the sound came from above, so I looked and saw a guard flying toward me, sword poised to strike. More importantly, a sword glowing with holy energy (which as I explained before will force me into purgatory)!

I felt the impact of his sword right behind me as I shoved myself through the temple wall and felt I had really been lucky to evade his strike, then felt my energy begin to burn away as I remembered I was inside a temple! I projected my voice to call for the woman who was supposed to be able to help us, bellowing, "PRIESTESS GILLIAN! MICHELLE NEEDS YOUR HELP TO ENTER THE CITY!"

I was happy to hear a startled sound from another room, which was enough response for me to finish the message with telepathy while shouting for her to meet me at the 'Chickenchair' Inn. While shouting that nonsense—which was strictly for anyone else listening—I directed my telepathy to seek out the person in the direction of the shocked gasp: <Ignore what I said about the Inn! Michelle needs your help and the guards are hunting me right now. Meet me across the street from the temple in two hours! ACROSS THE STREET-TWO HOURS!>

The few other robed ones there were regarding me with shock as two guards burst into the temple. In the same moment I pushed through the wall into the street to the side of the temple and hurried away, guards in pursuit. I was feeling weak because I had phased through so many walls, but I finally moved underground to avoid the devoted guards. I was impressed and annoyed by the tenacity and speed of the guards. When you have nothing to do, two hours can seem to stretch into days. As I had learned to do long ago, I zoned out. In about half an hour I blinked into consciousness again, though.

I had wondered how people slept with all the noise and it occurred to me that although I was in the temple for only a few moments the sound from outside didn't penetrate it's walls. That was a handy thing to think of for the buildings in the city—a way to seperate the noise outside from those who were sleeping inside. I very carefully moved back to the alley across the street from the temple and waited. When it was finally time, three hooded figures left the front door of the temple. I was about to curse when I saw that each one left in a different direction, one of them headed straight toward the alley.

When I pulled myself out of the ground there was the same shocked gasp as before. Smiling and raising both hands in a gesture of nonaggression, I sent the telepathic message, <Hello, I'm very pleased you got my message. Telepathy is pretty easy to use, just picture your message and 'push' it to me. I'll catch it.>

I still couldn't see her face, but the hood she wore nodded in acknowledgement and I recieved a response from her, <Is Michelle safe?>, She sent me.

I nodded, smiling, and sent our plan to Priestess Gillian along with the main points of interest: Her party meeting up with us, Hebbeth dead, Lizard army siege, reverse summon. It took the priestess a minute to sort through the details I had given her. A disturbed frown tipped me off that she wasn't entirely satisfied with the plan. "Deceiver!", She hissed, backing away and holding out a holy symbol in between us.

Then she called for the guards.

I was already moving away when she called a second time and I heard boots slapping the street louder and louder as they pursued me. It's easy to evade those chasing you when you can pass through solid material. "I hope that Nigel's choice is more helpful than the priestess was.", I grumbled to myself while hiding. I wasn't certain how long my comrades would be able to stay undiscovered and figured that the worst thing Nigel's pick could do was call the guards who were already hunting me, so I headed in the direction Nigel had told me I could find the home of the mage trainer. I found the building easily thanks to the handy sign above the shop. As I neared the place, I noticed that the words on the sign changed every few seconds to tout the different types of supplies that were available. I approached the door, preparing to phase through it, but to my surprise the door opened as I neared. When I crossed the threshold of the doorway a few soft chords played out, announcing my prescence to those within. The door gently closed behind me as a man looked at me over the rim of his spectacles. Severals lamps burned in the place, giving good light. None of the lamps had any oil in them, but they continued to burn, heedless of the fact that they defied explanation.

The aged man turned his focus back to the project he was working on, bowls of powders and liquids filling most of the table and a few pieces of small, but complicated machinery taking up the remainder. He was constantly pouring or moving the pieces and sometimes he would cast spells. Without stopping his actions, he asked in a kindly voice, "What are you looking for?"

I smiled at his nonchalant attitude. It couldn't be often that he dealt with an apparition. I explained, "Well, I had an idea for an unusual project and would like some assistance in testing it out."

He didn't bother hiding his interest, "Well, the unusual does interest me. What did you have in mind?", he asked. "I was thinking of using a summoning gate as a portal for people to . . . bridge distances.", I told him.

"The cost would be greater than the cost for a portal spell or a teleporation spell, but it wouldn't be able to be stopped as easily.", he said. It sounded like he was considering the proposed experiment aloud, but I suspected he was hinting at the fact that the reverse-summon gate would make it easy to bypass popular wards against teleporting or portals. For instance, into a city that is defending against besiegers. I was about to explain more of the situation as to why I was doing this when he said, "Alright. Let's try it out." and then bellowed, "STUDENTS!"

I cringed on that word. "These students are well-versed in summoning?", I asked, quite certain that this was turning into a bad idea. "Most definitely not.", he chuckled. "They wouldn't be interested if it was the same old thing—my students love to learn new things! STUDENTS!"

I heard what I was dreading: The pitter patter of little feet. A young girl and boy came down the stairs, Sleepy-eyed and yet ready for a new lesson. The two stopped and marvelled at me. Their eyes flew open and the little boy said, "WOAH! He's a ghost!", in amazement. Making their way more slowly down the stairs, two young men took in the situation. One smiled as the other's brow furrowed. They were all so . . . young. The first two couldn't have been more than ten years old and the older two were probably in their mid-teens. The middle-aged man was already ordering them around and my doubts began to disperse as the four students quickly and efficiently cleared an area and gathered the supplies their caretaker rattled off. In five minutes they were already busily working on setting up the wards and symbols for the summoning portal. I stayed out of sight of the door in case anyone came checking for me, but we weren't interupted.

Some of the supplies were used for other projects, though. Some of the things he had told his students to do seemed unrelated to the task at hand. When one of the teenagers noticed my confusion, he laughed and finished what he was doing (wrapping a long thread of green cloth around the handrail on the stairs and casting an enchantment on it), then explained what was going on to me. "Earl is a kind man,", he told me quietly, "though at times he's just strange. Everything he does has purpose, even if it's for something entirely different. His mind works on many ideas at the same time."

I kept my voice low out of respect, but I asked the young guy, "Is his mind alright? He's not going to set us all on fire or anything, right?"

Before I finished asking, the boy was already shaking his head, "We are definitely safe when dealing with his projects. I'm guess he just thinks on a higher level than we do. You know, I've never seen him sleep." The boy was thinking to himself for a moment and then snapped out of it. "Oh, I'm sorry. Anyway, I'm Bradley.", he extended his hand, then realized he was trying to shake hands with a ghost and put his hand back down sheepishly. Bradley pointed to the other older boy and told me, "That's Bart—he had a tough time before he came here, but he's coming around." Indicating the boy and the girl, he said, "That's Victor, he's been here since he was a baby—he's a handful!—and she's Tara."

Suddenly serious, he said, "To be honest, Tara has better magic than any of us do. She's only been training for a few years, too. She'll definitely be famous someday!"

Earl and Tara were the ones who were starting the spell to open the portal and hold back any evil entities. The little girl was providing more power for the spell than her elder was! There was a crack as if some universal law had snapped in two and the gate ripped open. Even a second is too long to stare into hell. Thankfully, the entrance gate that Nigel and Michelle had set up found this corresponding exit gate and the two linked, leaving only three feet of hell between them and us.

My comrades huddled together, their hands bound behind their backs and lizardmen soldiers clad in armor pressing the points of their spears and swords close to the bodies of my friends. I sent my friends the telepathic message <I'm sorry! We can't let the lizardmen overtake the city!> and shouted at the young mages to close the portal!

They responded surprisingly quickly except for Earl, who was over at his work table writing down notes about the reverse-summoning portal. The lizardmen started forward, batting the demonic tentacles and claws aside and slicing them off to get through. The portal began to shrink as the students neared completely shutting it. A barbed tendril whipped around and slashed right through the little boy's shirt, lifting him off the ground and throwing him onto his back a few feet away. He groaned in pain and got back up. It was a nasty cut, but didn't appear to be deep enough to have seriously harmed him. Tara took a few steps back for safety—smart girl—the same tendril would have lashed her as well if she had stayed put. "It's almost done, finish it and I'll get our blades!", Bart told Bradley. He then turned and bounded up the stairs two and sometimes three at a time. The portal was down to the size of a wagon wheel when a huge claw poked through it. Then all three of the kids panicked. "AUGH OH NOOO!", Bradley backed up quickly, pulling Tara with him. The claw opened wide and did a short sweep to knock away anything near the portal, which was nothing at this point.

Bart came back down the stairs and handed Bradley a short sword and gave a dagger to Victor. His own sword was already bared and he stepped toward the scaley grey claw bringing his sword to the left and slashing across to his the back of the claw. It left a scratch but otherwise clanged off as if it had struck another sword. Bradley, although he had sounded panicked, had regained his composure with lightning speed and unsnapped his scabbard, sliding his sword out and simultaneously throwing his scabbard out of the way as he stepped up and prepared to deliver a blow to the claw. Victor edged up but had no reach with the dagger. The claw swiped again to hit anything near, but all three of them backed out of range.

Then it began to push back and forth, and to our horror the portal began to stretch further open! Before the others got near it again, Tara unleashed a powerful lightning bolt that exploded a chunk of scaley flesh from the gigantic hand. The claw stopped struggling a moment and opened in shock and pain. As the moment passed, it curled into a menacing fist, promising retaliation. Still curled into a fist, it resumed jerking back and forth to force the portal open again. Tara stood back and began charging another lightning bolt. Earl told her, "That was an excellent lightning bolt, little one, but remember I said no magic attacks in the house. Go on outside if you want to train your attacks."

I stepped to the side of the claw and pushed into it to drain energy from whatever it was while Bart and Bradley took turns slashing at it, trying to hit the wounded part. Each time they did it would pause for a moment.

It wasn't enough, though. The portal was soon bigger than it had been initially and a second claw joined the first and simply pushed the sides of it wider. I drew all the energy I could, but it still didn't seem to be waning at all. The huge head of a dragon stared threateningly through the portal and when it had made the portal wide enough it crawled through, followed closesly by our friends who were held hostage and a large group of lizardmen. Bradley turned to Victor and Tara and told them to run for help. Even as they turned to go the dragon told it's soldiers, "If they leave kill the hostages and everyone that remains, then catch the one who ran."

Tara was holding the lightning energy behind her back and the dragon looked around at us. "Who wounded me?", it demanded to know. Bart snarled laughter and stepped up to the dragon's face, then whipped back his sword and—was cut down by four swords and two spears. Bradley shouted in despair and leapt forward, chopping halfway into a lizardman's neck and grabbing the spear it had been holding. The other soldiers stepped forward and Bradley drove the spear into the face mask of one of them. It jerked and fell backwards making terrible sounds. Weaponless, Bradley turned and ran toward the rows of shelves in the workshop. I was draining energy from one of the lizardmen when the dragon cast a spell that trapped me in a bubble. I knew how Slop had felt when it had been caught in a bubble, now. Bradley grabbed a large red jug with a skull and crossbones painted on it and wasted no time in uncapping it. He held it at arm's length, which implied it's very proximity was unhealthy.

The dragon's claw snapped forward and wrapped around Bradley, then began to crush him. "Humans. Evil comes so naturally to them, combat so easy. Death is what they want, and that is what they will get!" The liquid oozed between the claws and sizzled. Bradley couldn't have breathed anyway, but the fumes must have been toxic, because his eyes rolled back in his head and he began to quiver. It was over mercifully quick, and the dragon dropped the body. Yet as he did, Tara cried out, giving voice to the tears that glistened on her face as she struck the dragon in the eye with her second lightning bolt. In crimson fury, the monster roared and shook the entire house. Shockingly fast, it stopped roaring and, it's good eye narrowed in anger, it plucked Tara off her feet and tossed her into *the open side* of the portal—into hell! "BREAK THE SPELL!", it snarled to the lizardmen on the other side of the gate. With a swipe of it's tail, the dragon broke the components of the spell on our side and the dimension breach repaired itself within thirty seconds.

While that was going on I noticed that Martin wasn't among my friends who were being held hostage, and Axer wasn't, either. In fact, Axer was ordered to murder Earl and did so—with the scaley soldiers laughing all the while—but Martin snuck out with Victor while the dragon raged, a scaled hand over the boy's mouth as he cried out for his friends. They were his only family. Although Michelle's hands were bound, she was still a powerful sorceress. She had not spent her time idly and I could feel the energy around her as it continued to build. Watching so closely I could tell she was trembling in her effort to contain all that energy. She had been gathering energy so quietly the lizardmen had overlooked it, though. The dragon cast a healing spell on himself, but his eye was gone. The spell shut up the wounded eyesocket so that it didn't bleed any more. As the healing spell finished, there was a blinding flash, and as the brightness faded the captives were no longer there except for me. As the scent of smoke and echo of a magical sound faded we came to realize that the captives had just been teleported.

Axer remained, Certanius remaining quiet, even telephathically, in case our thoughts could be overheard by the dragon. Obviously the other lizardmen were uninterested in the arcane arts or mental aspects, so the dragon was the only threat in that regard. What an immense threat, though! The dragon growled and the reverberations rumbled the whole house. Soldiers were gathering outside, and with a thunderclap and a woosh of air, a magical dome flashed into being around the house, effectively trapping the lizardmen. The dragon reared up, attempting to stand on it's hind claws. When it struck the barrier and couldn't overpower the spell, it screamed in frustration and began weaving a spell of it's own. Outside I saw some mages concentrating on keeping the barrier up while a smaller group was scrambling to prepare a *VERY* powerful spell. "PREPARE TO ATTACK!", The dragon commanded his large squad of reptilian soldiers.

They quickly obeyed, forming up into a wedge and brandishing their spears, axes, and swords. Outside, the human guards of De'Lujean also took stances, readying themselves for the fight of their lives—not against the lizardmen as much as Sissoks, who towered above all others. The intensity in the air kept growing as the race for magical energy continued between the ancient dragon and the mages outside the shield. The strain was showing on the mages, but the dragon wasn't slowing at all. One of the mages holding the shield up kept looking at a sorcerer who appeared to be in charge and was helping with the other spell. The mages were beginning to visibly shake as they tried to contain all the energy they could, the energy gathering slowing even more. Their opponent still drew in more and more mystic energy and I could see the problem. His body simply had more mass than the mages' bodies did. The more mass, the more energy that could be held. If you hadn't known who to look at you would have missed the head wizard nodding to the shield mage. At that moment the barrier mage shouted a command and at the same time the spell-chargers and the dragon both unleashed a torrent of magical destruction at one another.

The beams of force collided with a mind-numbing crash and the two streams of energy pushed against one another. The shield mages were gathering their strength for a different spell while the dragon was spending it's efforts against the magic attack of their brethren. However, the huge dragon's energy was overpowering the attack mages! Guards were swarming in to disrupt the dragon and destroy it's squad, and the lizardmen moved forward in unison to challenge the brave guards. The numbers were closely matched, but as the fight was taken I lost hope. The guards were fighting one or two at a time, and the lizardmen kept a tight line, assisting each other in eliminating the defenders. The shield mages began casting spells to strengthen the soldiers, and the tide began to shift. Ever so slowly, the lizardmen were being forced backwards by guards who were protected by magic. Where blades would have punctured flesh and rended bone, they were now deflected!

The dragon took note of that as well and gave an extra push, beating it's enemies' stream of energy back until the dragon's own beam hit those standing in the path, slamming them in all directions. The dragon stopped providing energy for it's beam and the remaining energy in the stream decimated a building. The dragon leapt into the air and began flying toward the main gate where it's army waited outside. <Certanius!>, I called out with my mind.

<Jordas, what is it?>, Certanius responded.

I told him, <I need your help to break free of this bubble! We have to stop the dragon before it lets the lizardman army into the city!>

There was a moment of pause and then Certanius let me know, <Axer is on his way.>

Axer had become one of the lizardman allies right away, so I was unsure how it would turn out. I still had the image of Axer leaping onto the table and planting Certanius' axe into Earl's skull. A disturbing image, but I'd seen it myself. On the other hand, if Axer had fought against the lizardmen or the dragon then he'd be dead now. Axer didn't seem to contemplate regret for the death of Earl. The dragon had dropped from the sky by the time Axer came running up. Without a moment's pause, the goblin leaped as high as he could (he probably would have been able to strike me in the shoulder) and brought the magic axe down on the bubble I was trapped in. The weapon itself was worthless against the bubble, but Certanius had spent all of his training learning to counteract magic spells as Hebbeth had been his target. I'm certain it took less than a thought for Certanius to shatter the bubble spell. <Which direction did the dragon go?>, Certanius asked after I had been freed. For Axer's benefit I spoke my response, "The dragon flew toward the main gate, that way!", I pointed even as I started in that direction.

Glancing behind me as I headed for the gate, I saw that the lizardman line had broken and they scattered throughout the city, killing anyone they could while escaping the enchanted guards. De'Lujean was quickly filling with shouts of triumph from the victors and the screams of their victims. One sound roared over the voices—it could only be the main gate of De'Lujean being destroyed. A tidal wave of victorious cheers flooded the air as the lizardman army began to pour into the jagged hole that had been blown open and which was now guarded by the dragon. Bells rang out in defiance against the invaders, and the masses of De'Lujean began to appear with every kind of weapon, from sharpened sticks to legendary swords. While the lizardman army might outnumber the guards, they had a distinct disadvantage against the population of De'Lujean, especially when the lizardmen were limited to the space near the gate, which removed their number advantage.

At the same time, most of the mages who had fought against the monstrous dragon had survived and regrouped, arriving behind the battle lines and preparing several seperate spells to kill the dragon. I hovered above the raging battle and stayed as far to on the edge as I could, avoiding Sissoks' attention. The mages unleashed their spells and Sissoks countered and fought back with his own spells. The mages had a slight advantage until the lizardmen began to break through the wall of defenders and a few of the mages were cut down by the excellent fighters the lizardmen had. I began drawing energy from Sissoks when I reached the massive opponent. He knew I was weakening him, but all of his time was occupied in fending off magical assaults. If the lizardmen kept defeating the De'Lujeans, though, soon the mages would have have no shield against Sissoks' warriors and the fight would be lost. Blue and red lightning bolts cracked the air, fireballs speeding this way and that, being repelled or absorbed. The havoc in the air matched the clangor of warfare below, blood spraying bright red, being loosed by dull and shining weapons alike.

The more experienced fighters of De'Lujean were being revealed now by their remaining prescence while others fell around them. The war was quickly being lost, we could tell. The moment the mages could no longer overpower the dragon, the fight would be ended. Sissoks was weakening, but the De'Lujeans were falling too quickly. I kept taking energy from Sissoks, but the dragon was drawing so much energy in that he had enough to spare for combat. As fresh soldiers continued to arrive for the lizardmen from the broken gate, my hope waned.

An electrical buzz drew my attention to an armored figure that glowed blue for a moment before looking around and nodding. Blue electricity sparked from his form as he lost his transparency. He kneeled and I could no longer see him. Suddenly there were more flashes of blue light as more armored soldiers appeared. The few who had come through took their place beside the De'Lujeans and began push back the invaders even as more teleported in. The lizardmen were having more difficulty with the heavily armored warriors and the battle turned in our favor. Two men appeared at once holding a large banner between them. I heard one of their soldiers cry out, "For King Aldrenni!", as he cut down a wounded lizardman. Other battlecries rang out as well, some shouting their causes, some crying out for blessings and others that were simply wordless roars of triumph. An arrow hit Sissoks' other eye, and he bellowed louder than them all as he staggered backward. In the blink of an eye a powerful lightning bolt tore through the middle of the mighty dragon's body, instantly killing him.

The corpse of the dragon twisted and fell sideways, crushing those who were beneath it and blocking the broken gate. Lizardmen caught between the wall of scales and the defenders were overwhelmed immediately, and cries of victory filled the air, for a short time replacing the stench of death and the pain of those who were wounded and dying. I was near enough to hear one of the De'Lujean mages ask how King Aldrenni had known they were in peril and why he had helped De'Lujean, a great city, but one that was not a part of his own lands?

The warrior who the questions were put to lifted his visor and looked solemn as he told the mage, "A debt long overdue had to be paid, and my liege finally got the chance to repay it. We were glad to help your people."

The knight removed his helmet and the cry came from the wall watchers that the lizardman army was moving away from the city into the wilderness. Many celebrated, and many also grieved. De'Lujean would live—they would rebuild. This, I realized, was the reason I had stayed. Somehow I had known that I would be needed to help weaken the dragon. Somewhere I'd seen a glimpse of the future. Though a dome covered De'Lujean, the light in the sky beckoned to me again. My work here was done. As I ascended into the light, time slowed for me. I was no longer bound by limits, and was free to view those I was seperating from for the time being.

Chapter 9

Looking into the future

As I looked down I first saw my friends. Elwin lead a peaceful life, training healers of the future. His greatest student was a pure soul, I felt. His name was Kahn and he became renowned for his ability to heal the most severe of wounds and even reverse death itself for a select few!

After seperating from us, Vincent returned to his home. He spent little time in his town because everything had changed. In the time he was there, he rooted out several corrupt officials and was able to get them charged for their crimes and replaced with better people. When he had completed that, he travelled across the continent to the opposite shore. During his travels he met many people who admired him, but never grew close to them. On the opposite shore he met another who shared his tendency to go wherever the wind took him. They became partners on a quest and decided to keep it that way, even though his partner was a man not of higher principles like himself. The man's nickname was Silver and he was a well-renowned mercenary. The nickname came from the color of his enchanted armor, and Vincent soon bought a new set of armor that was imbued with enchantments and runes to slow down his aging and protect him in dangerous times. He began to go by the alias of Copper, and together the duo accomplished many dangerous missions together. Years later, they took up residence as guards in a shop run by a familiar face.

That familiar face was not pretty. Even a handsome goblin is not very nice to look upon, and after years of healing the scars left on Axer's face made him a less-than-handsome goblin. Between Axer, Certanius and

Martin, the lizardman army imploded on itself in less than a year due to internal problems caused by information that was leaked and the lack of evidence to find out who the spy was. Most lizardmen were killed and those who survived after the army disbanded had a difficult time in a world full of hate directed at them. Martin actually created a link between lizardmen and humans by providing work for the poor on his farms. Martin did enjoy his life and lived it out as a lizardman. His legacy was that the lizardmen were able to exist without being hunted down in the world.

After the army disbanded, Axer returned Certanius to the hidden headquarters of the Knights of Irbogronth's Hidden Eye. Axer was rewarded with a powerful magic item, an indestructable hammer, and a book of rare magical spells. Certanius' body was restored to him and he joined his family. For many years he spent part of his time aiding his fellow knights in seeking out problems and solving them, but never again accepted so difficult an assignment as hunting Hebbeth had been. Though not a peaceful life, Certanius was satisfied and happy. The knowledge he left in the books he wrote are still among the most important in techniques of meditation and counter-magic.

Axer took a ship and sailed to other continents, learning about sailing and trade. He had taken to calling himself Konco after he had received the indestructable hammer, but after several years, he sold his indestructable hammer to a wealthy man who ran an immense oceanside kingdom. Although the hammer went, the name stayed, and he used the money to buy up valuable artifacts and items and open Konco's shop. Having read the rare spell book, Konco enchanted his shop with a spell that very few understand. From outside, his shop appears to be the size of a normal building, but when one crosses the threshold of the door it's obvious that more space is inside than out!

Nigel and Ferrin stayed in contact through a pair of magical rings they had for years. Ferrin eventually travelled to Crescent Isle—where Kahn made his home—and helped to heal thousands of terrible afflictions. Nigel, as I suspected, had been the one who had called in a favor from the prince he had once rescued. Michelle and he had been planning (using telepathy!) ever since they were captured by the lizardmen. Michelle had teleported everyone to the King Aldrenni's homeland—the prince's father had been assassinated, making him the new ruler—and Nigel had alerted them to what was happening and the grateful king had not made his champion beg. The armored knights were teleported all the way to De'Lujean to fend off Sissoks' army. Despite her great power in sorcery, Michelle died very shortly after the teleportation. In teleporting everyone such a long way she had overextended herself and sadly caused her own death. Her sacrifice saved tens of thousands of lives, though.

Nigel met an unfortunate fate only months later when, questing into a dungeon, he was tricked into a trap by a succubus. The trap was a floor that fell out from under him, dropping him into a deep underground lake. If he hadn't had so much equipment he would have been able to swim. I could see, though I could not help him. In his last panicked moments, realizing his terrible mistake, he activated his ice rings and then touched them to his fire rings. The resulting mystical detonation froze the entire underground cavern solid. That change affected the climate of the entire area, even aboveground. I couldn't see further into the future, but I could sense that his soul was not yet free. Someday someone would find him and bring him back. By that time Ferrin had returned to his elvish homeland and was saddened that he could no longer contact Nigel, but he was happy to be amongst his people again. Ferrin was not so special among his people, who knew much magic and were wise in the ways of meditation and transcendesence. He fell in love with a beautiful elvish girl and they led a charmed life as far into the furture as I could see. I had the feeling that someday Ferrin would be the one to find Nigel since he put the ring away in a safe place.

Will stayed in the Aldrenni kingdom after Michelle died. I did not see the end of his life, but I was granted the knowledge that long after he passed on, philosophers would be studying his life. What I could see suggested that his life would continue on it's current path, soaking up every bit of knowledge like a sponge drinking water and helping others by way of taking on the challenges that few were able to. He never did become attached to anyone although at times he tried. His was a path of understanding . . . and loneliness.

Clay survived for years thanks to his skill in combat and his tactic of running away if his allies got into too much trouble. In one such situation, though, a few survived after he had left them to die. They found him and exacted their vengeance in a most unkind fashion. His family mourned him even though the manner of his death did not surprise them. His older brother, who had been born crippled, saved up money and hired an assassin to kill the three who had executed his sibling. The assassin completed the job and a short time later the elder brother fell out of a window. Rumors swirl that the same assassin was hired by one of the family members of the first victims of the assassin in order to retaliate upon the cripple. A tragedy that had many chances to be avoided. Only the most dedicated of scholars will find records of Clay 'Sharptongue', and the only memory lies in the battles he helped to win.

More renowned for being less savory was Drake. The cleric of a violent order of anti-evil teachings, I was able to more clearly see his true nature as I ascended. Drake was vile. A hypocrite who profited from the suffering of others. He deceived often and for selfish reasons and was eventually trapped and made to suffer himself by some very cruel demons. Instead of being tortured to death, however, Drake became a demon himself. His name isn't able to be written, not because of the generally difficult nature of demonic names, but because his primary focus is on deception and destruction. Though time and again given a chance to change his ways, eventually a holy quest was given to remove that diabolical soul. The chosen one that the quest was given to carried it out and then faded into obscurity—partly because of the demon's nature of deception, but also due in part because the hero themselves did not wish wide recognition for their actions.

Simon wasn't as old as I'd thought—in spiritual experience, anyway. He didn't have an easy life, but he didn't gain as much experience as he needs, so although I got to spend some time with him he's planned a return trip to get up to speed. Not all of us need to return, but some have to come back more than a couple of times! Keep an eye out and maybe you'll see an old habit he had. Well, the only habit he had was keeping quiet most of the time, so maybe you won't notice him. He's okay, though.

Out of everyone we encountered, the most interesting story had only begun because of our adventure. After Tara was tossed into hell by Sissoks, Martin saved the young boy, Victor, by hiding him in a safe area of De'Lujean. Martin left, and Victor was left alone, save for his love, Tara, who he knew was not supposed to be in hell. Finding no help in De'Lujean, Victor travelled to several cities where renowned sorcerers and magicians lived to find help in saving Tara.

His studies under Earl had been magical as well, but Earl had focused more with machines when teaching Victor because the boy had a natural skill at understanding their workings. Since the arcane was not as well known to him, he tracked down those renowned mages to ask for their help and information. When those who taught him found out his true reason for learning about their arcane arts, they stopped teaching him and he became known for asking help for his extremely dangerous quest to save Tara from hell. Oddly enough, the ill repute he gained actually attracted necromancers and death mages to him. He found much more help from those mages than he had from the others he had asked for help from. The price was more dear, but without his love he felt there was no point in his existence, so he made every sacrifice with little thought. The only thing he refused to give up was his own future, his own safety. He knew his pain at being seperated from Tara and never wished her to feel that way. In his hurry to save Tara he rushed every preparation, but his luck held and in less than half a year's time he opened a portal to hell itself to save Tara.

During the time he had spent trying to learn more, he had been penniless and had stolen everything he needed to survive. Before he left into the portal on his quest, he decided to steal everything he might need to succeed. This fact wasn't very important on it's own, but later it's relevance would become clear.

Not only did Victor fight with demons, he dealt with them. In everything he did he remembered not to be tricked into giving up his own life or soul so that he and Tara could be together in the end. The details of his quests were never documented in the material plane, but he eventually was able to find a way to restore both Tara and himself to the material plane—alive! Tara's life had turned into a savage nightmare from the moment she had been cast into the hell gate. Like the details of Victor returning them both to life, the details of her torment was clouded to my vision—though I feel it was more to spare me unnecessary pain in that regard as opposed to the details of Victor restoring their lives, which was not supposed to be done.

The demon he dealt the most with had declared it's name to be TubSleh. Backwards (as most demon names are) it's name actually was Hell's Butt! After successfully returning to life both of them were scarred, but finally together. In hell Tara had not been abused the entire time—her arcane knowledge had been put to the ultimate test. Her previous potential grew into a truly astonishing level—it had to be in order to fend off the horrors that approached her. Between Victor's knowledge of machine and necromantics and Tara's ability in elemental magic spells (Air, Water, Earth, Fire) they built a tower for them to live in. Tara could not stand to be around other people. Her experiences had made her paranoid of anyone else. Victor tried to find work but was shunned everywhere he went. A mark of the unnatural had been placed on him for coming into the material plane from hell, and several orders of clerics made it clear far and wide that he was not to be dealt with but openly attacked.

As he had previously, Victor stole what his love and he needed to survive. Together they fended off attacks on their home. As time wore on Victor's attitude changed more and more. Why should they be made to suffer so much? In Victor's mind it was their turn to be happy after all they had endured, and it was the rest of the world's turn to suffer! Stealing had become a habit for Victor, and it grew into an unmanagable beast. He began to dress up and call himself the Mechamancer, using his skill and knowledge of machines and the dark arts to steal whatever he and Tara needed *AND* whatever they wanted. Anyone who tried to stop him was met with an unwavering front of cold cruelty. Tara grew restless on his outings and Mechamancer did what had always worked for him—he stole for her. When you steal a sentient being it's usually referred to as slavery, though. Since Tara couldn't stand other people, he brought back four goblins. The goblins obviously ate well and were happy to live with them. Neither Victor nor Tara were unkind to them.

Victor himself grew tired of leaving the tower to pillage what they needed or even in fending off attacks. He set traps to destroy those who dared to attack them and also set machines and golems to work guarding them. He raised the corpses of his enemies as zombies and sent them to steal for him as well. Tara could actually sense the scrying that was done to find out more about the tower and grew quickly afraid of them. Using her incredible powers, she whipped up an enchantment for a self-sustaining storm a mile in every direction of the tower. The whipping wind and falling water ruined any spell used to look for them. Hell's Butt, in repayment, was granted every effort Victor could make to resummon him every time he was destroyed. Hell's Butt acted as a commander away from the tower and, obviously, guarded Victor and Tara with every life he had. The two managed a comfortable existence though they went about achieving it in a dark way. Their story will continue and has much to offer, so look for the writings detailing the lives of Victor and Tara and the way their lives and the lives of others near them changed. The best record is titled, "Mechamancer".

Little is left to tell. My own existence ended on the material plane and I was allowed into the eternal kingdom. I really am not supposed to give *this* much away, but it is as they say: If you open your eyes you will see, but no amount of proof is enough if you choose not to see. Currently I'm spending what I can only describe to you as an infathomably long time enjoying the company of those I love the most. It's not easy to do the right thing, but it's worth it—so be good!

Ah, I almost forgot. On a deep level of Hebbeth's dungeon there's a soul that borders *just* on the edge of sentience. I called it Slop, and although the name fits right now, someday it won't. Just so that you know, Slop is still alive and enjoying it's life far below the surface. Slowly it's gaining mass and will, at some point, understand it's place in the scheme of things.

Don't worry, eventually you'll understand your place, too.

Special Thanks to

God, for giving me more than I could ask for.
Mom, incredibly selfless and hardworking.
Dad, strong and smart and still humble.
Andy, steadfast and honest.
Nick, a newfound old friend and fellow writer.